I'd never done any of the things COUNTRY GIRLS in MY BOOKS did, because I wasn't one of them. I was a CITY-IN-THE-WINTER/ RESORT-IN-THE-SUMMER GIRL. The closest I ever came to "COUNTRY LIFE" was driving past McMURTRY'S FARM.

But all that was about to change, because I'd never had a SUMMER OF FREEDOM before. And I'd never met anyone like THE GIRL I'd seen STANDING IN THE CORN.

Swing
SIDEWAYS

NANCI TURNER STEVESON

HARPER
An Imprint of HarperCollinsPublishers

Swing Sideways
Copyright © 2016 by Nanci Turner Steveson
All rights reserved. Printed in the United States of America.
No part of this book may be used or reproduced in any manner
whatsoever without written permission except in the case of
brief quotations embodied in critical articles and reviews. For
information address HarperCollins Children's Books, a division
of HarperCollins Publishers, 195 Broadway, New York, NY 10007.
www.harpercollinschildrens.com

Library of Congress Control Number: 2015955158
ISBN 978-0-06-237455-4

Typography by Erin Fitzsimmons
17 18 19 20 21   OPM   10 9 8 7 6 5 4 3 2 1
❖
First paperback edition, 2017

For my sons, Parker and James—my reason for everything.
And for Javier. Fight on.

ONE

Mom's voice flew back at me from the front seat.

"Annabel. Did. You. Eat. Your. Sandwich?"

Staccato, like six birds hitting the windshield, one right after the other. My arm jerked, knocking the foil packet off my makeshift writing desk. I caught it before it fell to the floor and wedged it between my thigh and the over-size suitcase taking up half the backseat. Dad gave Mom the Hairy-Eyeball Look.

"Vicky, stop."

"I only wanted to know if she'd eaten it so I could throw the foil away for her," she said.

"She can throw it away herself."

Mom turned and studied the dense trees off the side of the highway. "I'm only trying to be helpful."

Stop being so helpful.

Dad reached over and squeezed her shoulder. "She'll take care of it. I'm pretty sure that's what Dr. Clementi meant when he said she needs freedom."

She dabbed the corner of her eye with a fingertip and kept staring out the window. "I'm well aware of what Dr. Clementi meant. No spreadsheets. No schedule. No Mom. All summer."

At our last family therapy session, right before the end of the school year, Dr. Clementi had dropped a bomb on everyone's plans when he'd said I needed a summer with "minimal structure, no spreadsheets, and lots of independent decision making." He'd said I needed freedom.

Freedom.

Just the way the word sounded made my belly flip.

I scrunched lower and doodled in my red Story Notebook. Maybe if I slid far enough down they'd forget I was there and talk about something else. Maybe they'd forget I existed and let me be.

"Come on now," Dad said. "No one said anything about no Mom. Just not the hovering one." He winked at her. Dad's a big winker.

"I said I would try, Richard. I'm trying." She pressed her

forehead against the glass.

As far as I could tell, nothing much had changed, and it was already the middle of June. Mom had waited until the last second to strip the final spreadsheet from the fridge door at home; Dad was still dancing between the two of us, trying to make everyone happy; and when I'd looked in the mirror this morning, the image staring back at me was still all angular and bony and hollow.

I pulled the waistband of my jeans together and stuck my finger in the gap to see if it was getting any smaller, to see if I'd managed to put on some weight. Not yet. Maybe, if I got my promised freedom over the summer, I'd get right in the head. Maybe I'd be able to eat without feeling like my throat was closing. Maybe then I'd look normal again.

A few miles later Dad tapped the rearview mirror. "Hey, Pumpkin, was the sandwich good?"

That was his way of supporting Mom and still showing he was on my side. Dr. Clementi said it's called "enabling," and apparently Dad's a master at it. I lifted the packet from the seat and peered inside. The whole thing was a slippery mess. Why would anyone make cucumber-and-mayonnaise sandwiches to eat on a four-hour road trip in the heat of summer? Why would anyone post-1960s make them, period? A white glob seeped out and dropped onto my lap.

"It's all hot and gross. I'll eat something else when we get to the lake house."

Mom sighed really loud, so Dad tossed a minibag of Oreos into the back.

"Here's something to hold you over. If you choose it, I mean." He winked in the mirror and put his hand on the seat behind Mom, belting out "All You Need Is Love" loud enough for anyone in the universe to hear.

Half an hour later we were off the highway, driving on the winding road that ends at the lake, when I saw a girl standing in the corn. Dad eased the brakes going around a big curve right before McMurtry's farm, only a mile shy of our summer home. People whispered about Mr. McMurtry. They said he was a recluse, that he'd gone crazy and his family had run off, leaving him to tend the place alone. It was hard not to believe them. Except for the manicured acres of emerald corn stalks lined up by the side of the road, I'd never once seen any sign of life on that farm.

Every year I'd ask what was wrong with Mr. McMurtry. Every year the answer was the same. "He's a hermit," Mom would say. Then she'd give me that you-know-what-I-mean look. But I didn't. So I always asked. "It means he lives alone and doesn't want to be bothered."

My eyes would sweep over the mess of vegetation hiding the house from the road. Tangled bramble bushes, waist-high weeds, and unpruned trees had been left to grow willy-nilly across the property. Seeing it always made me ache to do something wild and crazy, like leap from the car and roll down the hill into the thick of it. An activity, of course, that would never make it onto one of Mom's spreadsheets.

"What made him that way? Where's his family?" I would ask.

"He doesn't have any family around, Pumpkin."

"But who takes care of his farm?"

"Apparently no one, from the looks of it," Mom would snip.

"Except for the corn." That was Dad. "He does take care of that corn!"

But this year there was a girl about my age standing barefoot at the end of the rows, every bit as tall as the corn. She watched us drive slowly past, hands propped on broad hips, and big, naked feet planted shoulder wide. Masses of yellow hair sprouted from the top of her head like a haystack. When she saw me hanging out the car window, my face wilting with envy, she dipped her head to one side and grinned.

If it had been anyone else I would have yanked my own head back inside, embarrassed at being caught gaping. But something about her reminded me of Dad's favorite word—*shenanigans*—like maybe she was getting ready to stir some up. My heartbeat thumped in my throat, and my fingers gripped the open car window. The girl rocked back and forth on her heels, studying me like she was trying to decide if I was up for the kind of mischief she had in mind. In my heart, in my soul, but silently—only in my mind—I screamed, *"Yes! Yes! I am!"*

Dad pushed the gas pedal, and the girl turned, watching us drive away. She got smaller and smaller and we got farther and farther until finally, right before we crested the top of the hill, she raised one arm and wiggled her index finger at me.

Come back!

TWO

D ad stopped short just inside the kitchen door. Mom careened into him, and I pitched against her back. All three of us gaped at the fridge where the last spreadsheet, from the last week of last summer, glared at us. No one had taken it down when we'd closed the house on Labor Day. No one had known it would become such A Thing. Now we stood silent, our arms full of pillows and musical instruments and tennis rackets, and no one knew what to say.

This is what Mom's spreadsheets looked like:

	MONDAY	TUESDAY
8:00 am	Practice flute	1/2 hour stretching
9:00 am	Breakfast	Breakfast
10:00am	**Tennis Camp**	**Tennis Camp**
4:00pm	Mom picks up	Mom picks up
4:30pm	Snack	Snack
5:00pm	Flute lesson	Gymnastics
6:30pm	Dinner	Dinner
7:00 pm	PBS	Stretches
7:30pm	Independent Study	Independent Study
9:00 pm	Read one hour	Read one hour
10:00 pm	Lights Out	Lights Out

WEDNESDAY	THURSDAY	FRIDAY
Clean room	Math Flash Cards	Cooking with Mom
Breakfast	Breakfast	Breakfast
Tennis Camp	**Sailing Camp**	**Sailing Camp**
Mom picks up	Mom picks up	Dad picks up
Snack	Snack	Snack
Private Tennis lesson	Math Tutor	Wise Use of Free Time
Dinner	Dinner	Dinner
Finish cleaning your room	Flute practice with Mom	Movie Night
Independent Study	Independent Study	Movie Night
Read one hour	Read one hour	Movie Night
Lights Out	Lights Out	Lights Out

And that was for one week in the summer. *In. The. Summer!*

"I'll get it." Dad lunged forward and stripped the yellowed paper from the door, cramming it under his armpit alongside a can of tennis balls. Mom's face turned pink, and she moved toward the stairs. A big white mark was left where the spreadsheet had waited all year for us to return.

"Huh." Dad swiped his arm across the fridge and blew away the gray dust on his sleeve. "Good thing the cleaning crew comes tomorrow." Then he followed Mom upstairs.

I studied the empty white space and swallowed back a one-second panic attack. The missing spreadsheet didn't make me feel independent and free, like I expected. It terrified me. *Missing* being the key word. Clutching my notebook and pen, I ran to my room and hid until dinner.

By the time the sun cracked the next morning open I was already dressed, perched on the edge of my bed, gathering the courage to sneak off to McMurtry's farm. The idea of showing up unannounced at a stranger's house was scary enough, especially one like creepy Mr. McMurtry. But if I didn't act quickly, Mom had the power to suck me back in and make me forget the whole Freedom Plan without me even realizing she was doing it.

At breakfast everyone acted like it was a normal day in the Stockton household, which, of course, it was not. Mom spread butter and marmalade on wheat toast, her face all scrunched like she was trying to sort out something in her mind.

"So, Annabel," she said, with a pleasant voice meant to disguise her real feelings. "What are your plans on this beautiful morning?"

She was trying to act nonchalant, but I knew what she wanted. She wanted to know exactly where I was going, and she wasn't supposed to pry. Dad shook open the *New York Times* and peered at me over the top. I cut my waffle into dozens of pieces and plowed little roads through the syrup— a trick I'd learned to make it look like I was eating—and tried to come up with something that wouldn't give away my real plan. Freedom or not, no one had to tell me McMurty's farm was off-limits.

"First, I'm going outside to meander." I let my mouth draw out the word *meander*, then pretended to concentrate on the waffle's journey, piling pieces into a small hill and smashing them flat so the syrup seeped out the little squares. Eventually the whole mess looked like it had already been through my digestive system.

Mom stopped spreading and repeated "meander" like she'd never heard the word before. Dad put his hand on her arm.

"Well, we have tons of errands. Let's hustle so we can get back before the cleaning crew shows up." He stood and cleared their plates. Mom was left holding her toast and the butter knife above her placemat. "Come on, Vic," Dad called from the kitchen.

Five minutes later they were on their way out the door, waving a list that should keep them busy for hours. Mom couldn't resist one last little instruction. "Don't forget the rules—keep your cell phone on, and send a text at noon."

I touched the new phone in my pocket, the one thing tying me to them until my noon check-in, and to six o'clock, when I was expected home. It was the only way she would agree to the Freedom Plan. Who was I to complain? I'd never had a cell phone in my life. Things could be worse.

When I was sure they weren't turning back, I grabbed the Story Notebook and jogged almost the entire mile to McMurtry's farm. Across from the orchard, I stopped and leaned against a tree, gulping in air to catch my breath. Other than watching from the car window, this was the closest I'd ever been.

Dad always said anyone could tell I was a country girl at heart from my bookshelf. The year I turned eight, when all my friends buried their noses in fantasy books, I'd read the entire Little House series—twice. My favorite part was when Pa made a ball for Laura out of a pig bladder. I'd asked Dad if he had a bladder at his biology lab at the college. Two weeks later, he'd slid a clear plastic bag across the dining-room table to me. Inside was a flat, pinkish-gray circle.

"As you requested."

Mom had stared like it was a bag of poison.

"It's all sterilized," Dad had said. "But I'd suggest you do your experiment out of Mom's sight." He winked, then cut a slice of roast pork and popped it into his mouth.

The next year, when I was nine, I'd read another favorite countrified book, *Judy's Journey*, about a poor girl whose mother made her a dress from a calico flour sack. I'd asked Mom if she could sew something like that for me.

"Flour comes in a paper bag, not a calico sack," she'd said.

Mom teaches calculus at the same college where Dad teaches biology, which is why by the time I'd read *Judy's Journey*, I already understood Fibonacci's number sequence and the natural division of cells. Still, her lack of imagination withered me.

"If you buy flour at a feed-and-hardware store, it comes in a calico sack." I held up my worn, orange copy of *Judy's Journey* as proof.

She'd put down her *Architectural Digest*. "Annabel, when was the last time you saw a feed store in Manhattan?"

"See? This is why we should be living in the country. Then we could make our own clothes and pick wild berries for dinner."

Mom had scrunched her forehead, which meant she was about to have a worried-about-Annabel moment. "Wild berries have bacteria. They can make you sick."

I'd stuffed *Judy's Journey* under my arm and stormed from the room. At dinner that night Dad had asked why I was so sulky. I put my chin on my fist and pretended to ignore him.

Mom had said, "She read a book about a poor girl and asked me to sew something from a calico flour sack."

"It's not only that, Dad," I'd grumbled. "It's that we live in a city. There's nothing good here—no grass, no ponies, no cows to milk or crops to harvest and sell. Nothing."

Dad'd tapped my head and smiled. "Pumpkin, you're the only privileged child I know who wants nothing more than to be poor."

"I'm probably the only nine-year-old on Earth who's never eaten a berry right off the vine."

Back then, I was sure it was true. I'd never eaten a berry from a bush; never brushed a pony's tail; never owned a dog, raked leaves into a pile, made jam, or picked pumpkins out of a patch. For all the years I'd helped Dad with Summer Science Camp at the lake, for all I knew about leaves-of-three and spores and how caterpillars digest themselves before turning into butterflies, I'd never done any of the things country girls in my books did, because I wasn't one of them. I was a city-in-the-winter/resort-in-the-summer girl. The closest I ever came to "country life" was driving past McMurtry's farm.

But all that was about to change, because I'd never had a summer of freedom before. And I'd never met anyone like the girl I'd seen standing in the corn.

THREE

Clumps of tiny green apples grew along branches that curled and jerked and reached far across the rows of the orchard, as if the trees were trying to shake hands with each other. Underneath, the grass was so high it fell over on top of itself. Past the orchard, a dirt paddock stood vacant against one side of a two-story red barn. For as long as I could remember, I'd wanted to get inside that barn. And now, here I was, standing across the road from the place I'd drooled over since I was big enough to see out the car window, and I was too scared to move.

What if everything people said about Mr. McMurtry was

true? Or worse? What if he'd tied his family up in his base-ment? What if he caught me spying and told Mom? Maybe the girl had only been my imagination. Maybe I was crazier than I thought. No, she was real. She'd wiggled her finger at me. Even I wasn't that crazy.

I took a deep breath, tugged at my shorts, darted across the road, and walked past the empty paddock, sniffing for any hint of a pony. With a barn and a paddock, there must have been ponies at one time: fat, snowy ponies with manes that fell to their knees and backs that sunk like cushy sofas. But not even a tuft of hay rolled by.

At the top of the driveway stood a red mailbox. No name, only a crooked, black number seven. I resisted the urge to straighten it. Spindly lilacs lined a gravel driveway, and a jumble of wheat-type stuff covered what used to be a yard. Peering around the corner of the barn, I squinted and stud-ied the place I'd coveted for so long, listening for the sound of someone lurking nearby. Silence. No sign of a human.

A path of flat blue stones led to partially buckled wooden steps and a covered front porch. I was so close, a few strides away from ringing the doorbell and asking for the girl, like a normal kid would do—if I were a normal kid. I could navi-gate the subway to and from school by myself, even in the winter when it's dark at four thirty, but the idea of walking up to this house and asking for a girl—a plain old girl—had my heart pounding.

Breathe in, breathe out. Breathe in, breathe out.

A twig snapped.

I gripped my notebook with sweaty palms. Dried weeds rustled from across the driveway. I pressed my back against the corner of the barn and held my pen up like a knife. The sound of footsteps moved closer. Was it the old man? Had he seen me? I stood my ground, braced to run, my attention trained on a spot where the weeds crackled and shook. Suddenly, the girl shot straight up from the thick of it all, holding one hand in front of her face.

"Shhh. Don't go up there." Her eyes were as big as dollar pancakes, the color of sugared blueberries. "He doesn't know I'm outside." She ducked low, poking only the top of her head above the weeds, and scouted quickly left to right. "All clear—follow me," and she was gone.

A man's voice cracked through the air so sharp it made my knees jerk. "Catherine?"

The New-and-Improved Annabel sprinted across the driveway and into the brush. I followed her down a path that twisted and turned and finally spilled me into a small clearing where she knelt, peering at something in her hand.

"He's calling for Catherine. Is that you?"

"Puh, no. My name is California." She raised thick eyebrows and hitched up one side of her mouth. "He thinks it's a hippy name, so he calls me Catherine."

"California," I repeated.

"Right. As in the state." She popped something into her mouth, then tilted her cupped hand toward me. "Just picked these, right off the vine."

Raspberries. She was holding a handful of real, fresh-picked, straight-from-the-bush raspberries. "Where'd you find them?"

"Down past the woodpile. There's an early crop starting to ripen. Want some?"

Mom would have a fit. I nodded, and it felt like a string that had been wound around my neck eased up.

"Come on then," she said. "Let's get more before he finds me."

She sprang away. The imaginary string fell from my neck and let loose something wild and careless. I ran after her, through a maze of brush and tall grass. We skirted the edge of the corn rows, ran past the house, and finally stopped by a large, shady tree where the ratty weeds gave way to a sloping field of soft, pale-green grass. It was the kind of hill that begged a girl to roll herself into a ball and laugh all the way to the bottom. Especially a girl like me, who had more opportunity to trip on museum steps than to tumble down a grassy hill on purpose.

On the far side of the tree, behind a neatly stacked pile of logs, a broken chain-link fence ran down the hill and disappeared into the woods. California headed for the fence. Thick vines with heart-shaped leaves wove in and out of the steel links.

"He doesn't bother with these anymore," she said, kicking aside a rusted watering can. "That's why there aren't a lot of berries. Raspberries need attention, someone to care for them. Like people. But we'll take what we can get, right?"

"Who's 'he'?"

California scrunched her forehead and ruffled her hands through the leaves. "That crazy old man is my grandfather, so if you want to laugh, or say something about how creepy he is, go ahead; let's get it out of the way."

For once in my life I had the good sense to keep my mouth shut. California reached down and yanked hard on a thick weed, jerking side to side until a spidery root popped out of the earth.

"I'll have to burn that sucker later so it doesn't creep back over." She tossed the whole thing by the woodpile. "Come on, take some for yourself. You know which ones to pick?"

When I didn't answer, she twisted a fire-engine-red berry from the vine. "When they're still this color, they're sour." She threw it down and gently pulled a berry the same ruby color as the stain on her hand. "This one's ripe. Try it."

I squished the berry against the roof of my mouth with my tongue.

"You like?"

"It's a thousand times better than chocolate."

She smiled wide, then pulled a navy-blue kerchief from her pocket and tied the four corners together to make a pouch.

"When you carry raspberries, you have to hold them like they're baby chicks so they don't get bruised—gentle, but firm." She plucked two and dropped them into the cloth.

"I've never held a baby chick."

"Yeah, I figured as much," she said, still picking. "But just imagine."

She walked along the fence pushing leaves away, squinting and searching for ripe berries. Half of them she ate, the other half she piled into the pouch.

"Have you ever held a baby chick?"

"Tons of times."

"Where?"

"Back home, in Oregon." She wrenched the fence upright where it leaned too close to the ground. "That's where I live. Now I'm here, for a while, anyway."

"For the whole summer?"

She shrugged. "Maybe. He says I'm going to school here in the fall, but I'm not so sure about that."

"Otherwise you go back to Oregon?"

California narrowed her eyes. "You sure do ask a lot of personal questions."

My face flushed hot. I couldn't go anywhere without everyone knowing when I was embarrassed. She didn't notice, just raised the berries up in both hands like she was weighing the bounty.

"That ought to be enough, don't you think?"

"Enough for what?"

"For you to take home. What'd you think I was pickin' them for?" she said, holding out the bundle of perfect, right-off-the-vine berries—bacteria and all.

Mr. McMurtry's voice cut through the air. "Catherine!"

California glanced toward the house and crinkled her nose. "Snap. He's going to make me do math all afternoon. I hate math."

"I can help if you want. My mother's a math professor, and I—"

"No, that's okay. Piper says I'm as good as any college kid. But I'm homeschooled, so Grandfather thinks I didn't get a real education."

She pulled the knot of the kerchief tight and patted the top, then tilted her head and studied me.

"There might be something else you can help me with, though. Something much more important than math."

"What?"

"We'll see about it tomorrow. It's an adventure. You do like adventures, right?"

Without waiting for an answer, she turned and disappeared into the brush. The weeds closed up behind her, and I touched my cheek to be sure I wasn't dreaming, that the girl was real and had actually left me standing on McMurtry's farm with a bundle of perfect raspberries in my hands, and the promise of a real-live adventure tomorrow.

FOUR

When I got home, the blue Volvo was parked snug against the steps. I dodged behind the rhododendrons, stuffed the last of the raspberries into my mouth, and ran to the deck where I could see through the sliding glass door. Inside, Mom and Dad sat shoulder to shoulder, bent over a big, open book spread out on the coffee table. Fabric samples. She'd already dragged him to the decorator. Dad had bribed her by promising that since I got my summer of freedom, she could redecorate the house. He flipped a page, she lifted a square of dark material from the binding, and they laughed together.

I wiped my face with the kerchief, shoved it inside Dad's and my firefly jar, and rolled it under the deck. The glass door swooshed when I slid it open.

"Hi!"

A big smile plastered across Mom's face plunged when she saw me. She leaped from the sofa, grabbed a wad of tissues from a box, and flailed them in the air, her voice rising at least two octaves.

"What's all over your face?"

"What are you talking about?"

"And your hair—" She reached for me, and I stepped back.

"I don't know what—"

She tugged my elbow and spun me around to face Grandmother Stockton's antique mirror. "You have a rash!"

A raspberry-colored stain circled my mouth. A long, thin smudge ran all the way to my left temple. My braids were loose, and bits of dried weeds clung to the ends. I groaned. Mom whipped us both around to show Dad.

"Richard—what is this?" She pressed the back of her hand to my forehead. "No fever, but really, one day in and already—this charade of a summer is not going to work if—"

She was right. This freedom thing wasn't going to work if every time I came home I had to go through an interrogation. I'd rather spend the entire summer holed up in my room. My jaw tensed, and the euphoria of my magical morning slipped away. I pulled at my T-shirt, positive I was about to choke to death right there in the living room.

Breathe in, breathe out. Breathe in, breathe out.

Dad jumped up, grinning. "Hey, you've been picking raspberries, right?"

"Raspberries?" Mom spit out, as if he was talking about illegal drugs. "Where would she be picking raspberries?"

"Behind the boathouse," Dad said. I took one tiny, hopeful breath. "Same bushes were there when I was a kid." He winked at me, then sat down and tapped a page of the fabric book. "Vicky, stop fretting over her. Come tell me what you think of this color."

She stood perfectly still, fingertips on my shoulder, like she couldn't truly let go in light of my pending Death by Raspberry. Dad jerked his chin toward the stairs.

"Go on, Pumpkin, get yourself cleaned up. Babe, what do you think about red? It might make a nice change from navy. My mother was always particularly fond of red for summer."

At the mention of imitating Grandmother Stockton, Mom released me and I bolted upstairs. I needed a bath. Fast. A hot bath would bring me back from the edge of a full-blown panic attack. My throat was already tightening. I sprinkled lavender beads under a stream of hot water and inhaled until the gripping sensation around my neck began to fade. By the time I sank into the tub, the panic was easing.

At lunch they talked nonstop about colors and fabrics and couches. Mom gave Dad a lesson in the difference between French Country decor and Country Contemporary decor. Dad nodded and smiled at all the right times, like he was actually enjoying it. Maybe he was, who knew? I didn't care because no one asked about my morning, and no one complained that I didn't eat.

The next morning Mom was in the kitchen packing food into a wicker hamper, her face bunched up tight like a ball of twine. Item by item, she arranged liver pâté, crackers, Camembert, red grapes, bottles of Perrier, and triangular packets of cucumber sandwiches deep inside the basket. Only my mother would take that kind of stuff on a picnic. I'd stopped letting her pack my lunch after fifth grade when Robbie Knight dipped his finger into my pâté and told everyone I was eating poop.

She smiled when I came in and automatically glanced at the refrigerator to check the spreadsheet. But there was no spreadsheet, only the blank, white door. Her eyebrows stitched for a second, then she forced a smile, as if it didn't bother her one bit.

"We're going to sail and have lunch with the Radcliffes. Do you want to come?" She held up a chocolate cake, as if the idea of eating cake might tempt me.

"No, thank you."

I opened the refrigerator and stuck my head close to the cheeses and fresh fruits. The back of my knees felt like someone had snapped a rubber band against them. Mom never expected me to say no to anything she suggested. The Freedom Plan was about to be tested.

"Where are you going?"

I shuffled strawberries and Brie around and pretended not to hear.

Dad sidled up and poked his finger in my side. "Tommy Radcliffe should be there," he teased. "Sure you don't want to come along?"

Tommy Radcliffe had been like my big brother since I was five and he was six. He'd been as predictable a part of my summers as Mom's spreadsheets. We'd gone to camp and sailed together, he'd taught me how to swim, and we'd played tennis since I was big enough to grip a racket. But on the last day of last summer, Tommy tried to kiss me. He'd lunged across the sailboat, his mouth all puckered up like he'd been sucking on a lemon. I'd shrieked and pushed him backward against the mast, toppling off my side into the water. The next day we said awkward good-byes and retreated to different corners of the state to start a new school year. So no, I didn't want to see Tommy Radcliffe. Not yet.

"No thanks." I pulled the pitcher of cranberry juice from the fridge. "Too hot."

Mom opened her mouth to protest. Dad stepped in between us and pointed to the picnic basket. "Vicky, that's fabulous— exactly the way my mother would have done it."

Her eyes flickered between the hamper and me. "It was your mother's basket. We always take it to the beach the first day."

"I know; good old traditions standing the test of time." He

draped his arm around her shoulder.

"Which is why I really want Annabel to go with us—"

Dad put a finger to his lips. Several long, uncomfortable seconds ticked by. Finally, she shook off his arm and turned away, mumbling something that sounded suspiciously like swear words. Dad gave me the thumbs-up.

"Have a nice day, Pumpkin."

FIVE

"Hey, girl, I'm up here!"

Three rows into the orchard, the leaves of a sturdy-looking tree jiggled. I climbed through the fence and went to the base. California sat high on a fat limb, swinging her legs, wiggling long, ugly toes in the air. Two chunky yellow braids hung down over a red shirt. She smiled like she'd been dinged in the head.

"Hi!" I said.

"Hey, what's your name?"

My name? She didn't know my name.

I could be anyone.

I could totally leave Annabel behind, reinvent myself on the spot. I could pick a different name, something adventurous, exciting. I could tell her I was a descendant of Amelia Earhart's secret love child, or an astronaut's daughter, or a child prodigy writing the sequel to *To Kill a Mockingbird*. I'd picked the name Scout from that book for the story I was writing because it sounded a little wild, and a lot brave. If I told California my name was Scout, maybe she'd think I really was both those things. Maybe I'd even become a little wild and a lot brave.

I squeezed the notebook against my chest. The name was right there, written all over the pages, trying to come out of my mouth. It almost did. I almost said it, but at the last second I caved.

"Annie. Annie Stockton." It wasn't *Scout*, but it wasn't *Annabel*, either. Step one. "What's your last name?"

She stuffed a section of orange into her mouth and dropped the peel to the ground. "Just call me California."

"Don't you have a last name?"

"You can make one up if you want." She kicked at the leaves with her bare toes. "Hey, you coming up here or what?"

Getting up in that tree posed a problem. There's a big difference between regular summer camp activities—the kind where you might actually climb a tree—and the Summer Science Camp Dad and I did together. I had no idea how to scale even the first branch.

"Is there a ladder?"

"A ladder? Haven't you climbed a tree before?" When I didn't answer, California swung her legs over the branch and shinnied down the trunk. "Where are you from, anyway?"

"New York City."

"Huh, a city girl. No wonder. Never mind; it doesn't matter. Watch me."

She puckered her mouth, scrunched her forehead, and wrapped long arms around the tree. Lacing her fingers, she braced one foot against the trunk and hitched her way up till she got to the lowest limb, easily swinging her leg over to straddle it.

"Come on; now you do it."

California made it sound like I could do anything she did. I lay the notebook in the grass, ignored my long history of clumsiness, and gave it a try. First problem was, when I reached my scrawny, much-shorter-than-California's arms around the trunk, my face pressed into the bark. I tried to grip the sides instead, but as soon as I put one foot up, my fingers pulled away and ripped my skin.

"Ouch!" Blood seeped from the side of a fingernail.

"Come on, try again. You can do it."

The New-and-Improved *Annie* Stockton took a breath and clawed at the tree. I lifted one foot, bounced a few times off the other, and pushed, imagining myself rocketing skyward to the nearest branch. Instead, I sailed back and landed in the grass with a thud.

"Oh, my butt!"

California jumped down and smacked a hand against her forehead. "Holy beans, you might actually be hopeless!"

"Wasn't it hard for you the first time?"

"Can't remember. I was climbing trees before I could walk." She grabbed my hand and pulled. "Come on, I'll help you. Stand there and hold on tight." She crouched behind me and leaned her shoulder against the back of my thigh. "Okay, put one foot on the trunk. On three you pull up and I'll push, 'kay?"

"I guess. . . ."

"One, two, three—"

She heaved her shoulder into me. I tried, I really did, but in the end we both landed in a jumble of arms and legs on the ground. California rolled away and laughed, bellowing great, big honking noises through her nose.

"Annie-girl, you're so skinny! You must not even weigh a hundred pounds right out of the river. I ought to be able to fling you up there myself. No matter, I have a better idea."

She hopped up and sprinted across the orchard, hurdled the fence, and disappeared into the barn. Moments later she called, "Found it!" and loped out holding a ladder over her head.

"Let's just get you up there this time." She wedged the ladder under a branch. "We'll have climbing lessons another day."

Being up in that tree was worth all the scrapes and

humiliation. The leaves made a canopy over our heads, chlorophyll green and breezy, with a perfect view of the paddock, the barn, and the road. No one could see us unless they were standing right underneath. I silently swore I would master the art of tree climbing if it took me all summer.

California settled on a branch. "You like?"

"I love."

"I thought you would," she said, obviously pleased with herself. "And no worries, we've got the whole summer to work on your climbing skills."

We sat without talking for a few minutes, which was nice. Like we were already good enough friends that we didn't have to talk—we could simply be. From my perch I could look up and pretend I was spinning inside a green-and-blue kaleidoscope, occasionally catching glimpses of red when a robin flew by. I never wanted to put my feet on solid ground again.

California jabbed my leg with her toe. "Hey, have you always been so skinny?"

So much for dreaming.

"Don't act like it's some big secret. No one has ankles that sharp unless they have some kind of weird metabolism, or if they're not eating right. See mine?"

She stuck out a thick, tan calf as big around as one of the fence posts. I curled mine under the limb.

"Don't worry, we'll plump you up like a Thanksgiving turkey before the end of summer, just you wait and see. Hey, do you know what kind of apples these are?"

I peered at the tiny green nubs, grateful she hadn't made me talk about eating. "No, but there are hundreds of different kinds of apples."

"Egg-zactly! Neither of us will ever see all the different varieties, unless we become appleologists."

"There's no such a thing as an appleologist—"

"I know, but there should be." California leaned back against the trunk and flicked her toes at the leaves. "Do you know what apple wood is used for?"

Apple wood made me think of Dr. Clementi's chess set. During my first two appointments I'd fidgeted and sweated in a big leather chair that stuck to the backs of my knees, trying to think of things to say. At the third appointment he'd had a chess set on the table between us.

"Do you play?"

Studying a gleaming knight, I'd nodded. "I can beat my dad."

Dr. Clementi had picked up a dark king and turned it slowly in his hand. "My grandfather carved these. The dark are mahogany, and the light are white pine."

I'd touched the top of a queen. "He must have had a super tiny knife to carve the jewels in her crown."

Dr. Clementi had run his finger along the board. "In between each square is a thin piece of apple wood from a tree on his farm. I loved those trees. The summer I turned twelve

I swung from my favorite limb, and we both crashed to the ground." He'd pulled up his sleeve and pointed to a faint scar. "Thirty-two stitches."

"Ouch. That must have hurt."

"There are worse things than stitches—like my grand-father's disappointment when he saw that limb lying on the ground. I never wanted to face him again." He'd leaned closer, like he wanted to be sure if I heard nothing else, I heard this: "But we can't always live up to everyone else's expectations, Annabel. That's something you should remember."

California prodded me with her toe. "Hey! Apple wood?"

"Oh, yeah, uh, carving. My doctor has a chess set his grandfather made. Part of it is apple wood."

"Doctor? What kind of doctor has a chess set in his exam room?"

"It wasn't an exam room, not really."

She raised her eyebrows. *And so?*

"It . . . it was in his office, where we talked." Blood rushed to my cheeks. I didn't have to tell her, but somehow I knew my secret was safe. "He's a psychologist."

"Ooohhh. Well, that's a relief."

"Huh?"

"Well, if you were sick or something, maybe I shouldn't be shoving you up into trees."

"I'm not sick, not like that—"

"Yeah, I get it. The other day when you were going past

the farm, you reminded me of one of those pointy show dogs who needed to be sprung from a cage for a roll in the mud. That's why I invited you back instead of mooning you."

The idea of California's bottom shining from the middle of the cornfield made me giggle. "You were going to moon me?"

"Considered it. Gets tiresome, watching all those cars slow down so people can stare at the mess Grandfather's made of this place. He says it's the summer people. I'm supposed to stay away from them."

"I'm summer people."

"I didn't say I was going to do it, did I?"

"Will you get in trouble if he catches me here?"

"Puh." She flipped her hand. "Grandfather won't know about you until I'm good and ready to tell him. He has no idea what to do with me, anyway. I knew that the first time he called me Catherine."

"Why does he do that?"

She sat up straight and squared her shoulders. Looking down her nose, she made her voice sound all proper. "Catherine is a polished, respectable name." In her regular voice she added, "I guess that means California is not."

I giggled, and she smiled. Mr. McMurtry seemed less scary. A little stuffy, like Mom, but less deranged than the man who supposedly ran his family off.

"Yesterday you said something about Piper. Who's she?"

"My mother."

"You call her Piper?"

"What do you think I should call her?"

"Like, Mom or Mother. I call mine Mom."

"Well, I call mine Piper."

"Do you call your father by his first name too?"

"I don't have a father."

"Oh, I'm sorry—"

"Sorry for what?"

"About your dad. Did he die?"

"Puh. Never had one, never needed one."

I pushed the leaves aside to see if she was laughing at me, but she stared back like she'd said peanut butter was made from peanuts.

"There has to be a father. There has to be sperm—"

"Yes, Annie, I know that." Her fingers drummed against the tree. *Tharump-tharump-tharump.*

"I didn't mean—"

She held up two fingers. "Two words: s*perm* and *donor.* Piper wanted a baby, so she found a sperm donor and had me." She pretended to peer over a pair of glasses, librarian style. "You do know what a sperm donor is, don't you, Miss City Slicker?"

I shrank back. "Of course I know what a sperm donor is. My dad is a biologist. I just . . ."

"Just what? Never met anyone whose life might have started in a petri dish?"

"Is that how . . ."

California let out a big laugh. "Nah, no petri dish. I was just testing to see what you knew, that's all."

Bam! A wooden gate behind the barn slammed. We both jerked. California put one finger to her lips and pointed with the other.

SIX

"Catherine? Catherine?"

A large beast of a man charged into the paddock hoisting a shovel in one hand and a black, whiplike thing in the other. He was big and scruffy, with a mess of shaggy, salt-and-pepper hair, worn-out overalls, and black boots that looked ready to send trespassers sailing all the way to town.

California mouthed *"Grandfather."*

I hugged that trunk so tight the bark imbedded itself in my arms. Mr. McMurtry strode from one end of the paddock to the other like a windup toy stuck on go. He stopped at the barn and poked his head in the doorway.

"Catherine?"

My foot slipped, rattling the leaves. Mr. McMurtry swung around and marched toward us, his boots pounding the dirt like a soldier. He leaned over the fence, a mere three trees from where the red cover of my Story Notebook stuck out in the green grass. Fat, bushy hair grew together into a unibrow over his eyes. He was so close, the only things separating us were a few scrawny leaves and the grace of God. The nearness of him made my stomach lurch.

He dropped the shovel against the fence, grabbed the other end of the black thing, and flung it through the air until it splat on the ground directly beneath me. The black thing coiled itself up like a rubber tire. Slowly, one end separated from the circle and the rest followed. A long, thin line slithered away into the grass.

A snake!

My fingers curled like a contortionist's. I pulled my knees close and squeezed my arms tighter around the tree. Mr. McMurtry picked up the shovel, searched the orchard again, and stalked out of the paddock, slamming the gate behind him. Neither California nor I moved until we heard car tires crunching on the gravel driveway. An old Buick turned out and crept slowly in the direction of town.

"Oh, DAMage—" California hit her fist against the tree. "Son of a biscuit-eater!"

"Did you see that? He was carrying a snake!"

She was already halfway to the ground. "I have to be sure she's okay."

"The snake? Don't touch it! That thing could be poisonous!"

California sprang through the grass, lifting her knees high in the air. After a few strides she swung a hand down and came up gripping the snake right below its head. The tip of its tail spun in circles. She held it up and grinned like she'd won a prize.

"She's okay."

My toes recoiled inside my sneakers. "California, drop that thing."

"Don't be dumb, it's just an old black snake that lives in the barn. Her name's Matilda. She's a good snake—she eats mice."

"There's no such thing as a good snake."

"Come down and meet her. She won't hurt you; I promise." To prove it, she nuzzled the snake's nose against her cheek. Matilda hung still, except where the tip of her tail continued to spin. I choked back bile.

"I can't, not until you throw it away."

"Oh, for the love of Mike, you don't throw away a perfectly good snake." She lifted Matilda's tail in her other hand and carried her off to the barn. When she came out, she thrust her knuckles into her hips. "Saved her once again."

"Where'd you put it?"

"Under the barn, where she lives. Come down, Annie.

Grandfather will be back soon. I have something really important to show you."

The impatient way California stamped her foot was the only thing that got me out of that tree—which, thanks to gravity, was a whole lot easier than getting up.

"Stop worrying. Matilda's gone, and I need your help."

She grabbed my arm and dragged me across the paddock into the barn, yanked me past two empty stalls and into a large room with a tarp-covered mound in the middle. Flecks of dust drifted from the ceiling and settled on stacks of old saddles, piles of leather bridles, and harnesses. Above us, tufts of hay poked out from corner beams where birds flew in and out. Cobwebs hung across the windows, thick as Spanish moss. There was a weird feeling inside the barn. It wasn't magical, the way I'd imagined every single time we'd driven past. It was sad, like *Beauty and the Beast* when the dishes sang about being of no use anymore.

California pointed to the mound. "That's an old carriage under there."

"A real carriage?" I took one step, and a bird whizzed so near I could feel the wind from its wings on my face.

"Barn swallows," she said. "Their nests are everywhere. If they think you're going to steal their babies, they'll have every swallow in the state after you. Come on, we're wasting time."

I followed her up a narrow staircase to a dusty walkway open to the room below. Halfway down she stopped at a door, stood on tiptoe to reach the ledge, and retrieved a rusty key. Wiggling it in the doorknob, she said, "I found this place the other day. There's something in here that's going to help me get Piper back to the farm." The door creaked open. "Stay here."

I had no idea what she was talking about, but she had promised adventure. I'd waited a lifetime for adventure. A minute later she motioned me inside. Light spilled through floor-to-ceiling windows. A polished wood desk and leather chair filled one corner. The floor was covered with a clean cranberry-and-blue Persian rug. The place was immaculate. No dust, no clutter anywhere. Like the rows of corn—order in the middle of chaos.

"What is this place?"

"Close the door and watch."

She went to a wall of shelves crowded with fake, green ivy and hundreds of books, ran her hand underneath the bottom, and stepped back. Slowly, one-half of the wall swung out until it stopped at a right angle, revealing another room the size of Mom's walk-in closet. The hairs on the back of my neck stood on end.

"Oh!"

California pulled the string of a single bulb hanging from the ceiling. A triangular table fit perfectly in one corner. On top was an old photograph in a silver frame and a rose-colored ginger jar. Beside the table, a rolltop trunk stood flush against the wall. Yellow light bounced off a brass lock.

"What the—"

She picked up the photo of a lady holding a baby in her arms and brushed her hand over the glass. "I think this is my grandmother and Piper when she was a baby."

Neither of them looked anything like California. Judging from the chair they were in, both the mother and baby were tiny, with smooth, dark hair and eyes.

"Piper left here when she was sixteen. I don't know why, because, good golly, she talked about this place my whole life like it was heaven."

"What do you mean?"

"Everything was perfect. She had a mother and father; my grandfather was rich. Still is, I guess. Not sure where he got the money, but Piper was their only kid. They gave her everything. She went to private school, and she had show ponies with her own personal trainer. They went to horse shows all the time and had a big, fancy trailer they slept in. She was really good at tennis and they had their own sailboats up at the lake, too. Plus they went on exotic vacations all the time."

"Just because they had money doesn't mean they were happy," I said. "She could have been miserable being the only child. Trust me."

"I know about the money thing, but whenever Piper talked about it, she always had this sad smile, like she wished she could have it all back. I figured her parents had sold the place, and that they were dead."

"She never said why she left? Maybe she made it up, like a fairy tale you tell your kids."

She opened the single drawer of the table and got another key, this one shiny and new. "This was no fairy tale. This was the real deal."

The key slipped easily into the lock, and the trunk popped open. I inched closer. The inside was divided by a wedge of wood right down the center. On one side was a box covered in cream-colored, horse-print fabric. The other side was filled with loose photos. California lifted out the box and placed it on the table. Opening the lid, she gently peeled back layers of yellowed tissue to show me rows of brightly colored horse-show ribbons.

"These were hers. She won them." She ran her finger around the fluted edge of a royal-blue ribbon and turned it over to read what was written on the back. "'Peaches, Large Pony Hunter, Darien, Connecticut.'" Picking up another blue ribbon, she read, "'Cream, Pony Jumpers, Manchester, Vermont.' They're all marked."

"If she was so happy, why would she leave?"

"I don't know."

She rummaged through a pile in the other side of the trunk and held up a framed photo of a girl wearing a black helmet and holding the reins of two ponies: a dark chestnut with a light mane and blue eyes, and a cream-colored palomino. Their coats gleamed, and their manes were braided into stiff bunches, like miniature soldiers lined up along their necks. The girl was holding two long, tricolor ribbons, and she was smiling.

California read the inscription. "'Margaret with Peaches and Cream, Large Pony Hunter Champion and Pony Jumper Reserve Champion—Lake Placid, July 1986.'" She tapped the glass. "I don't care what they called her, that's Piper. This must have been taken right before she left. And she sure looks happy to me."

"Can't you ask your grandfather?"

"Puh, sheesh, no, I can't even say her name around him without his face getting all weird. There must be some reason she never told me, something really bad. I'm not going to ask. Not yet, anyway."

Her eyes shadowed over, leaving me with an uneasy feeling.

"What matters is that she needs to come home, and I might have figured out a way to get her to come back, before it's too late."

"Too late for what?"

She put the picture and ribbons back in the trunk, shut the lid, and edged me out the door. "Let's get out of here before he catches us. I'll tell you the whole story. What I know, anyway."

SEVEN

California led me down the same path we'd run along the day before, but instead of ending up by the raspberries, she took a turn into the thick of the corn. Fat stalks with shiny, green leaves lined up in precise rows. Young ears of corn, inside pale-green husks, had threads of yellow silk peeking out the top. California plopped onto the sandy earth between two rows, sending a puff of pale dirt into the air.

"Grandfather had cancer," she said. "He's in remission, but they're doing some kind of drug trial to see if they can be sure it doesn't come back. Or something like that. That's why I'm here, to help him 'cuz he feels puny after the treatments."

Her eyes shifted away. "I guess with cancer you never know if it's going to come back or if it's spread. It would break Piper's heart if they didn't fix what's broken between them if it came back."

"What do you mean, 'what's broken between them'?"

She picked up a clump of dirt and crumbled it between her fingers. "I didn't even know I had a living grandfather until we were coming here for the summer. They can barely be in the same room together. When we first came, Grandfather met us in New York City. They hadn't seen each other for a bazillion years, but they didn't hug, or smile, or anything like normal people do. One time I went out to walk the block around our hotel. When I came back, he was in our room. I could hear them arguing from out in the hallway. They started yelling something about me, so I left. By the time I got back he was gone, and Piper acted like nothing was wrong."

"She didn't say anything about it?"

"Nope. We met Grandfather at the hospital the next day, rode in the same train all the way up here, and neither one of them said a word until he dropped us off at a hotel in town. Then he just said dumb stuff like 'Do you need help with your bags,' and 'I'll be back to pick her up in the morning.'"

"Is Piper still here?"

"She left to stay with a friend in the city a few days ago." She threw another clump of dirt hard against the ground. "She was in town for three weeks and didn't come near the farm. After everything she'd told me my whole life, I wanted to know this place for myself. I asked her to come, but she said it was better for me to get to know Grandfather without her here. She probably figured she'd ruin it for me if they were angry all the time."

California wiped her eyes with the inside of her wrist.

"That's why I think my plan will bring her home. But I can't do it alone; it's going to take both of us. Will you help me, Annie?"

She reminded me of Mom when she'd wanted me to go to the beach. Like if I said no, she might break in two.

"What's the plan?"

"We have to find those ponies. If we do, we can make this farm like it was when she was a kid, when it was good, before whatever happened, happened. She'll want to come back to that place. I know she will."

It wasn't logical, but I couldn't ignore her eager-puppy face. "Would they still be alive?"

"Ponies can live thirty-five years, sometimes more. So yeah, they could still be alive. And I know they'd be here somewhere. I feel it, Annie. It's like they're waiting to be found."

"Here? On this farm? Wouldn't they be in the paddock, or the stables? Wouldn't your grandfather know?"

"Not if he let them run free after she left. There's six hundred acres on this farm. Do you know how big that is?" She flagged her hand in the direction of the lake. "That's like a giant chunk of New York City."

I quickly did the math in my head. "It's actually equivalent to almost one square mile, which is less than one percent of Manhattan."

As soon as I said it, I wanted to grab the words out of the air and swallow them. Not only had I shown what a super dork I was, it was argumentative, something smart kids should always avoid when in the process of making new friends.

"Uh, the point is, Miss Smarty-Pants, it's a lot of land for two ponies to hide. Besides, there's a whole thousand acres of national forest attached to it, so what percentage is that? Huh?"

It was seven and a half, but I wasn't about to say it out loud. "I get it. It's a lot."

"Right. Which is why I can't do it alone."

"You really think she'd come home for the ponies and not because your grandfather could get sick again?"

"I *know* it, Annie. If she could just remember what it was like before she left, I know she'd come home. I can feel it, can't you?"

The correct answer was yes, but I didn't feel it. It wasn't rational to think we'd find two ancient ponies on all that land by ourselves, just like it didn't make sense Piper would come home because of them, no matter what California believed. But the promise of adventure, of running through the woods and searching McMurtry's farm for two mystery ponies, was exactly what I wanted for the summer. I couldn't have got a better offer if I'd invented it myself.

"Okay. I'll help you."

I slid into my seat just in time for dinner. Dad winked like we had a big secret and scooped a mountain of casserole onto his plate. "You must have done more than mere meandering today, huh?"

My stomach growled at the aroma coming from the dish bubbling over with macaroni and cheese. Mom made it the way I liked it best: from scratch, with Gruyère, Cheddar, and Stilton, all "swimming in a roux" of sherry and buttermilk— she loved to say "swimming in a roux" like Julia Child—and topped off with a layer of grated Parmesan so it turned brown and crispy.

A few years back she had tried to teach me to cook. Her macaroni and cheese was the main thing I'd wanted to learn to make, but after months of scorched scrambled eggs and overcooked roast beef, she finally gave up. "I'd advise you to start saving money now so you can hire a personal chef when you grow up. Otherwise you should buy stock in tomato soup."

I smiled at Dad and dumped a heaping portion onto my plate, banging the spoon on the china. Mom shifted in her seat.

"I'm happy to see you eating, Annabel, but please remember your manners. And I believe Dad asked you a question."

"Well, that's the thing," I said, trying to make my voice strong and firm. Instead, it came out loud and shaky. "I changed my name to Annie today."

Mom's fork stopped halfway to her mouth. "Excuse me?"

Dad waved to shush her, and she shot him a piercing look. She hated to be shushed as much as she hated the Hairy Eyeball look.

"That's interesting, *Annie*," Dad said. "Am I still allowed to call you Pumpkin?"

"Well, yeah, that's a nickname."

Mom smoothed the edge of her place mat with her fingertips. "Your name came from my favorite grandmother. Why would you want to change it?" Dad reached over and patted her arm.

"Lots of kids change their names, babe. You can't take it personally."

"I just want to be called Annie. That's all."

Mom squeezed her eyes tight until her lashes disappeared, and chewed fiercely on her pasta. Her jaw clicked so loud she practically drowned out the hum of the ceiling fan. Finally, she took a sip of water and swallowed hard enough to down a croquet ball. Dad and I glanced at each other and turned back to our dinner.

For the rest of the meal I pushed macaroni around my plate and pretended to ignore the glares firing across the table. My parents spoke louder without words than they ever did with them. Dr. Clementi had warned me the summer rules would be hardest for Mom. He'd also said it was not my responsibility to help anyone except myself.

That night Mom clomped loudly up the stairs the way she did when she wanted the entire universe to know she was upset. The clomping stopped outside my door. My rocking chair sat next to it, with the quilt she'd sewn draped across the arm. *Annabel* was stitched in perfect, pink script along the border. A worn copy of *Winnie the Pooh* lay in the seat. When I was small enough to sit in Mom's lap, she read to me every night. I loved the way her voice rose and fell in time to the rocking of the chair and the way her arms circled me, the book open in her hands, so the three of us—me, the book, and Mom— became one.

I knew she was standing in the dark right now, thinking about me, probably wishing I was still small enough to wrap in her arms. Small enough not to want to change my name from the one she had picked. I pushed the fleeting moment of guilt away and whispered into the dark, "Annie Stockton, Annie Stockton, Annie Stockton."

EIGHT

"Keep pushing!"

I gripped the handles of the wheelbarrow and heaved again. California and I were deep in the woods, and a web of tangled vines had clawed its way around the wheel. I couldn't push through, even with her pulling up front.

"Oh, boogers." She dropped the front end and pulled a pair of giant shears out of a tool belt buckled around her waist. "Let me cut more of this crapola out of the way. We need to get through this last part to get to the river—"

Snap! A tight vine broke, and half the web fell away. She stomped heavy boots on the brambles and rolled a half-rotted log over them. A flurry of salamanders disappeared under last year's fallen leaves.

"Come on, I'm starving. I brought lunch. For both of us."

California had found the perfect hiding place for our supplies to search for the ponies. I was every bit as excited to get started on our sleuthing adventure as she was determined to bring Piper home. The river wasn't huge, not like the East and the Hudson Rivers in the city. It was more a wide creek. On the bank, an oak tree as big around as California and me standing side by side rose from a sandy dip in the earth, its branches canopied over the water. I put my head inside a hole in the trunk.

"Smells like smoke, like the one in the book about the kid who ran away and lived on the mountain."

"*My Side of the Mountain*," she said. "The hole is perfect for storing our stuff. That's *egg-zactly* why I picked this spot."

We unloaded an armful of old halters, ropes, a notebook, pencils, and a throwaway camera from the wheelbarrow and stashed them inside the tree. She pointed to bags of carrots and apples, and a rusted-yellow coffee can.

"All those go into that plastic bucket. Snap the lid tight. That'll keep the deer out."

I did as I was told. The day was so thick with humidity, I could barely see through the sweat dripping into my eyes. "It's so hot."

California pulled off her boots and dumped the tool belt on the ground. "Come with me."

I followed her to the edge of the river where clusters of rich, green ferns hung from the sides, their roots woven tightly into the earth. The soft fronds draped over a short drop to the water, which rushed by, clean and inviting. California crouched and wove her hands through the foliage.

"There's an herb growing in here somewhere that might help you." I knelt beside her. "I know it's here, if I can—" She raised one foot and, with a loud grunt, shoved hard against my hip. I opened my mouth to yell, flailed my hands in the air trying to grab hold of something to keep me from falling, but it was too late. My whole body toppled down the side of the bank, elbows and knees digging a rut in the earth, until I met the water face-first. My feet found the bottom, and I pushed off, shooting above the surface, coughing so hard that water spewed out of my nose. California stood on the bank grinning like a Cheshire cat.

"I can't believe you did that!"

"You said you were hot."

"What if I didn't know how to swim?"

"Guess I woulda had to save your life. Here I come!" she cried, right before cannonballing into the water.

When she came up, we laughed like we'd known each other forever. Like she'd been my best friend since nursery school and not Jessica Braverman, who ditched me last fall when the panic attacks started. Jessica had traded our friendship for contact lenses, a nose job, and her first crush, while I hid in the school bathroom every day, gasping for air. The blooming connection between California and me made my heart lift. It was a powerful feeling.

She stuck her toes above the water and spread her arms wide. I tossed my soaked sneakers onto dry ground, knowing I'd have to find a way to clean them before I got home. Rolling on my back, I floated beside her, forgetting about dirty shoes, and fake friends, and choking, and watched the sunlight push through the leaves overhead and sprinkle dapples across my belly.

"Piper used to sing this song about Peaches and Cream and fields of green and memories from long ago—have you heard that song? Because I never knew for sure if it was a real song or one she made up, and now I think, since I discovered the ponies named Peaches and Cream—well, since I found the photograph of the ponies named Peaches and Cream—now I think she made it up. It's a sad song; it goes like this . . ."

She warbled a few bars of something so off-key I dipped my ears below the surface to drown out the sound.

"She must miss them," she said when I resurfaced. "I'm not sure how she got all the way to Oregon by herself, but somehow she ended up on that tree farm building a yurt when she was seventeen."

"What's a yurt?"

"You know, a yurt." She pushed her legs like a frog, and her wiry hair spread into a yellow triangle on top of the water. "A thing you live in."

"I've never heard of a yurt."

"Didn't you study Mongolia in your fancy city school? Never mind. It's a dwelling. It's round with a pointed roof. Anyway, Piper helped build that first yurt. Then Harvard and Euberthia helped build one for her. We live in a permaculture community. It's better for the environment."

"Who are Harvard and Euberthia?"

"They're like my aunt and uncle, only not related. Harvard's mother named him that because they were so poor she knew he'd never go to college, so she gave him a name that sounded like he did. Isn't that a hoot?"

"Hoot? You sound like my dad."

I'd never heard of permaculture, had no idea what a yurt looked like, and wasn't even positive California was telling me the truth about either one.

She turned on her belly and swam to the side. "Come on, let's eat."

I scrambled up the bank behind her and squeezed water from my shirt and hair, pushing away thoughts of Mom's expression when she saw me. If we were going to spend a lot of time in these woods, I'd have to figure out a way to conceal the evidence. Mom had never once hidden how she felt about Mr. McMurtry—my friendship with California had to stay secret.

We ate sandwiches of homemade wheat bread and hummus. They weren't too bad, and there was no hint of throat closing, even with California staring at me.

"That's a start," she said, handing me a brownie. "Nothing like a day in the woods to build an appetite."

She had found a barrel of oats in the carriage house—further proof, she claimed, that the ponies were still around. After we ate, she swished the oats around inside the coffee can.

"Annie, think. Why would Grandfather have oats? Do we have chickens? Donkeys? Goats? What else might eat oats beside the deer he spends all year trying to keep away from his corn?"

"Ponies?"

"Yup." She smelled inside the can. "And these aren't twenty-year-old oats, either. I bet he feeds them in the winter when there's no grass. I bet they come right up to the barn."

We sprinkled the oats in between clumps of ferns and along the path we'd made to the water, and threw the apples and carrots farther into the woods. "If they find these, they'll come back for more."

Sealing the food inside the bucket, she set it beside the tree and smiled at me. "I really wish you could see yourself."

"Why? What?"

"Let's just say no one will have to guess where you've been today."

I followed her out of the woods, plucking burrs and dried leaves out of my hair and off my clothes. When we got to the bottom of the orchard, she said, "Picked clean as a cotton field in November," before turning away and zigzagging the wheelbarrow up the hill to the house.

I wiped sweat from my face and trudged past the apple trees to the road. The whole walk home I kept along the edge of the woods so I could hide if Mom and Dad drove by. About halfway I checked my cell. Six messages flashed on the screen. All from Mom. **Where are you? It's past noon!**

I'd missed my noon check-in.

I quickly texted back, **Sorry! Phone died. On my way.**

I should have signed it *Liar*.

NINE

Over the next couple of weeks California came and went, traveling into the city for her grandfather's treatments, and to meet up with Piper. Even though she was gone a lot, I still hadn't sailed with Dad or lost my yearly tennis game with local prodigy Deirdre Maxwell—and I was actively avoiding Tommy. My trips to the beach were quick, long enough to be able to say I'd been there, which kept Mom and Dad from asking too many questions.

On the Fourth of July, we drove into town to watch fireworks and ride the Ferris wheel at the carnival. The whole night I was jumpy, scared we'd bump into California and her grandfather in line for the next ride, or at the cotton candy booth. Mr. McMurtry didn't sound like the fireworks-and-carnival type, but they'd been gone a few days, and I wasn't sure if they were back yet or not. It would be awful if we ran into them. I'd never told California I was keeping our friendship a secret. That would require explaining why.

Most other evenings Mom and Dad were either busy working on the redecorating project or off at some friend's house to play bridge. I stayed home and kept my head in the Story Notebook, adding colorful, new details to the saga of Scout and the wild horse she'd named Liberty. Our summer was so out of whack, Dad and I hadn't even spent an evening catching fireflies.

What I had done was hide extra clothes, a hairbrush, and a tub of Handi Wipes inside the oak tree. Every time we were in the woods, I changed first thing. When we were done, I changed back, brushed anything woodsy out of my hair, rebraided it, and cleaned up with the wipes. And I never forgot the noon check-in again.

One night during the second week of July, we were eating lemon meringue pie for dessert when Mom said Deirdre Maxwell had been sent away to a tennis camp for kids "with potential." It was no secret my lack of athletic skills disappointed her, like I was doing it on purpose. Dad winked, scooped the meringue off his dessert, and dumped it on the side of his plate.

"Guess you won't have to play her this year, Pumpkin.

Maybe you won't have to play her ever again. Wouldn't that be nice?"

Mom frowned, then took the silver server and dished up her own piece.

"Yup. One less thing to worry about." I tucked into my pie, trying to figure out how to sneak a hunk of it from the house for California. "Thanks for making this dessert, Mom."

She was trying to do nice things for me. Twice she'd gone into the city and come back with bags of new summer clothes, the kind I actually liked. She'd been cooking all my favorite foods and had even left fabric samples on my bed so I could pick new curtains myself. I hadn't told her yet I didn't like any of the choices.

"Hey, the fireflies are out tonight," Dad said. "How 'bout we all sit outside and catch a few?" He looked from Mom to me, a lump of lemon curd on the fork hovering near his mouth.

"Sounds great, Dad. Can I have more pie first?"

Mom turned her dessert plate so the flowers on the border lined up evenly with the ferns on the place mats. "I'm glad you're eating, but be careful. You don't want to overdo it and get fat."

My head flew up as fast as Dad's fist pounded the table. "Vicky!"

Mom's mouth dropped open. The whole room vibrated with the electricity of a brewing storm. Impulsively, I grabbed the whole pie off the table and fled. Their argument was in full swing before my bedroom door slammed.

Later, Dad and I sat on the edge of the deck with the firefly jar between us, watching tiny lights dance around in the dark. I twirled the lid, and Dad wrung the cloth left over from the Raspberry Stain Incident in his hands. Mom sat alone in the living room playing Pachelbel's Canon in D on her violin. The notes drifted out the window, sad and sweet, with each pull of her bow. Dad turned his head to listen.

"You and Mom always played that together," he said.

"I know."

"One of my favorites. You haven't had your flute out all summer."

I shook my head and picked at the little holes we'd poked in the jar lid. "Pachelbel always makes me feel a little lost."

"Mom says when the two of you play together, it makes her heart swing sideways."

"She told me."

"You and Mom make my heart swing sideways. That's how much I love both of you."

I ran my finger around the edge of the jar lid. The music stopped inside. Dad waited, listening for it to start again, but it didn't. He bumped his shoulder against mine.

"Well, enough of the mushy stuff. Did I ever tell you that fireflies are nocturnal beetles?"

"Yup."

He smiled, then held the rag to his nose and sniffed. "Did I also tell you the best raspberries I ever ate grew on McMurtry's farm?"

My neck tensed. "Nope."

"Huh. Wonder if they're still there."

"Did you know them? The McMurtrys?"

Dad watched me for a second. "Everyone at the lake knew them."

"Why didn't you ever tell me that before?"

"I don't know. Does it matter?"

"No, I guess not," I said quickly. I wasn't ready to reveal my secret about California yet, not even to Dad.

"Changing the subject here, but you know Mom doesn't mean to make you crazy, right?"

I jammed the lid onto the deck. "I'm not going to get fat from one piece of pie, Dad. All that time I couldn't eat she kept shoving food at me. Now she's trying to force me the other way around."

"She worries when you're gone during the day and we're not part of it. We're used to spending the summers together, as a family, and now you're off on your adventures by yourself. It's not easy. We haven't even been to the beach together. Not once." He knotted one end of the cloth and swung it in circles. "Cuttin' the cord, letting the baby bird fly from the nest, it's really different, but it's especially hard for Mom."

"Why is it harder for her? Why does she have to be all

spreadsheet-y all the time?"

"Oh, I don't know, Pumpkin. Probably has something to do with the way she was raised. I always figured she became a math girl because math is orderly, and her life was so crazy after her dad died. Balance, you know? She wants your life to be more stable than hers."

"Dr. Clementi said parents do that. Mess up their kids because they don't want them to go through what they did, but they end up making different problems. Anyway, we're supposed to be doing the Freedom Plan, remember? If I want five pieces of pie, I should be able to eat five pieces of pie."

"I know. And Mom's trying. She really is." He watched her through the glass door, packing her violin into the case. "Sometimes I catch her looking out the window after you've gone off for the day, and I know she's wishing she could be with you, like it was before."

"Are you using guilt on me? Dr. Clementi said parents do that, too."

"Boy, he isn't going to let us get away with anything, is he?"

The light from the living room dimmed.

"You know Mom'll never stop trying to control me if you keep fixing things when we argue."

"Me? Where'd that come from? Oh, wait, Dr. Clementi again."

"He said when I was ready to handle Mom on my own I would have to tell you. He said that was how I'd feel safe, or something like that. I can't do it when you're always running around trying to make everyone happy."

"Since when is it bad to want everyone happy?"

I couldn't answer, so I shrugged, feeling like I'd stabbed him in the gut.

"Huh." He turned to watch the light show going on in the yard.

"Sorry. I didn't mean to sound that way," I said.

He handed me the knotted cloth. "Are you ready now? Is that what you're saying?"

"No. I don't know. Maybe. Sometimes. Not really."

"It's okay, Pumpkin. I get it."

Did he get it? Did I? Was I ready? All I knew was that I'd hurt Dad's feelings and had to make it better.

"I have a new friend," I blurted out.

"A new friend? What's his name?"

"Don't be dumb, Dad. It's not a boy."

"Oh, okay. Is it a secret?"

"Kind of." I lowered my voice. "It's Mr. McMurtry's grand-daughter."

His head jerked, ever so slightly. "Mr. McMurtry's grand-daughter. Who would have thunk it?"

"Did you know he had a granddaughter?"

"Nope, I did not know that."

"Her name is California—as in the state."

"California? That doesn't surprise me." He smiled funny, like he was the one with the secret. "Maybe you'll invite Miss

California over for supper sometime?"

"I don't know. I just want to keep it to myself for now. You can't say anything, Dad. Mom might say mean stuff about her grandfather. Promise?"

"I don't think—" he started, and then changed his mind. "Of course, top secret."

TEN

Watching California wolf down two pieces of pie the next day confirmed I should not invite her for dinner unless Mom was far, far away. She wiped yellow curd off her face with her forearm and licked the spot like a dog.

"Who ever figured you could make something so spectacular from eggs and a few lemons."

"I can't believe you've never had lemon meringue pie."

"Well, I can gar-un-tee you, I'm going to learn how to make it. That was the most deeeelish thing ever." She spit a lemon seed into the dirt, scooped it up, and stuffed it into her pocket. "Testament to the use of real lemons."

"How's your grandfather feeling?"

"Fine."

"Is he—"

"Annie, we're not talking about it."

"I'm sorry. I didn't—"

She waved her hand. "We can't get distracted from finding the ponies."

I groaned inside. What had started as an adventure a few weeks ago was beginning to feel like a punishing chore. For all the hot days we'd spent tromping through the woods, leaving food everywhere and documenting everything in the notebook, we'd had no luck. We scattered oats; they disappeared. Apples, carrots—same thing. Not one hoofprint, not one trace of pony manure left behind. Only a few mounds of pellet-sized deer droppings.

"Darn deer turds," California had grumbled.

The hotter the days got and the farther we trekked with no sign of anything pony-like, the bossier California became. Some days it felt like I'd traded a controlling mother for an equally pushy friend. It was getting tiresome. I packed the porcelain pie dish into the paper bag.

"I was thinking," she said. "Let's go around the edge of the field today instead of searching the woods. Grandfather wouldn't plow through snow on the hill all winter to feed a couple of ponies. He'd make them come get it. There's got to be a path, other than the one we made."

She led the way out of the woods and turned left where the tree line met the fields. The grass on the hill swayed in soft, pale-green waves. Down where we walked it was tangled with brush, sticker vines, and three-pointed foliage that looked suspiciously like poison ivy. The ground was cluttered with rocks the perfect size for ankle turning.

"If we find their trail, we're gold," California called over her shoulder.

We stumbled along for another five minutes. At least, I stumbled. It felt like a boot-camp exercise. Or torture. California marched. Barefoot. Her arms swung back and forth. Her bare calves plowed through anything in her way, whipping thorny branches back at me. The July sun stretched its flames close to the earth. The hair on my arms turned crispy. Crickets chirped nonstop. Sweat dribbled down my neck, soaking my T-shirt, and every chigger in the county was happily sucking fluid out of my ankles. With each swat, I prayed they weren't creeping into my underwear.

Apparently, California was immune to sticker burrs, heat, and chiggers. She stormed ahead, oblivious of my agony, yakking away like she always did about how she just knew we would find the ponies soon, and her mother would come and be reunited with her grandfather, and they'd all be so happy, and blah, blah, blah. It's all she talked about. *Ever.* I needed a break.

"Hey! I was thinking," I shouted.

She turned, eyebrows arched almost to her hairline, her eyes narrowed and suspicious. "About what?"

"I dunno. It's so hot today, and I'm all itchy. Maybe we could search somewhere cooler."

"Like where?"

"Inside the barn, maybe? It's always cool in there."

"What do you think we would find in the barn we haven't already discovered?"

She was irritated by my lack of enthusiasm for traipsing across an open field on the hottest day of the year. The taste of salt from sweat licked off my lips, and the burn on my shoulders only let me think about one thing: a cool, dark space to sit until my head stopped pounding, no matter what excuse I had to invent to make it happen.

"You found those ribbons and the photographs. There's got to be more of Piper's things somewhere. Maybe we'd find clues to something else that would make her want to come home."

"What *things* are you talking about?"

"You know, like a treasure box. Doesn't Piper have a treasure box of the pictures you colored when you were little, and report cards, and school pictures? Maybe there's one here for Piper, from when she was a kid. Maybe we should expand our search."

"A *treasure box*? What are you, five? And I'm homeschooled, remember? School pictures are just plain old pictures."

I was too hot, too thirsty, and too cranky to give in. "Wouldn't it make sense that your grandfather kept Piper's report cards?"

California shrugged and turned away, batting at a thin sapling that flipped back and barely missed my sunburned legs.

"I don't know where anything'd be, and I don't know what kind of clues you'd expect to find in a treasure box," she grumbled, air-quoting the words *treasure* and *box*. She marched forward with shoulders flung back, military style. From behind, she looked every bit as pigheaded as Mom, which did nothing to ease my irritation.

"California!"

She swung around and glared.

"I'm too hot," I said. "This is crazy. We need to go inside."

She thrust her fists into her hips. "No! We need to concentrate on finding the ponies. That's the only thing that's going to bring her home." Tears sprouted and dribbled quickly down her nose.

"I just thought—"

"Don't think!" she yelled. "Just do what I say!"

Another chigger sank its proboscis into my leg. I slapped my calf and scowled at her. "I don't know what you're so upset about. I told you I'd help you find those stupid ponies. I just think we should try something else while we cool off. Since I'm helping you, I should have a say in how we do it."

"Stupid ponies? Is that what they are?" She flung her arm at me. "If that's what you think, I don't need some smart-butt city girl who carries around a notebook like it's a binky to help me do anything. I was only letting you come along 'cuz I felt sorry for you!"

The Story Notebook burned in my hand. The paper bag with Grandmother Stockton's china pie plate shook. My mind went blank, and the back of my knees dropped. When my breath came back, so did my anger.

"Did it ever occur to you that I might be tired, that I might be hot, that I might need a break? I'm just suggesting that we could discover something new that would bring her home, something besides the ponies. Maybe he sold them, and we'd find out who bought them and could try to get them back. There are a million possibilities, you know. Not just one. But forget it. Forget the whole thing. See if this smart-butt city girl ever brings you lemon meringue pie again."

I threw the paper bag to the ground. Hard. Then, to make sure she got the point of how mad I was, I stomped my foot on top of it. Twice. Until I heard a loud crack. I stared at the mauled bag. "See what you've done?"

Her mouth opened so wide I could see all the way to her epiglottis. It was big, and rubbery, and wiggled furiously. Her cheeks puffed out. The whites of her eyes turned red, and dark circles appeared underneath. She clenched her fists, and her face got rounder, and tighter, and redder, until

I envisioned steam rushing from her ears and her brains exploding right out of the top of her head.

I had one foot back to step away when she puckered her lips and let out a long whoosh of air. Her skin faded to pink, and she squeezed her eyes tight. Her shoulders sank, her fists unclenched, and her jaw went slack. When she opened her eyes, they were wet. She spoke in a teeny-tiny whisper.

"The truth is, Annie-girl, I need you. I need you to be my friend. You don't understand. . . ."

My vocal cords were playing Ping-Pong in the back of my throat, so I kept my mouth shut. She wiped her face with the inside of her elbow, picked up the bag, and held it out.

"I'm sorry, okay? I'm scared. Every day we don't find the ponies, I get more scared. Sometimes I can't sleep and think if I ran away, she'd be forced to come back. They'd have to look for me together, but then I'd miss the treatments, and that's the whole reason I'm here, so I can't do that—I mean I couldn't go with Grandfather to his treatments. So I don't know what to do."

I stuffed the bag under my arm. One of the broken edges of the plate ripped through the paper and dug into my side. I needed to get out of the heat, and away from her words that cut sharper than the broken plate.

"Please, Annie, don't leave." Her voice cracked. "Let's go to the river to cool off. We'll make a new plan, just like you said. We'll look for something else."

She looked so pathetic standing there with tears staining her face, begging me not to give up. I couldn't walk away when she needed me like this, not like Jessica had done, no matter how hot it was. I nodded and turned toward our path to the river. This time California followed me.

We decided to search the rest of the barn, plus the attic and Mr. McMurtry's bedroom. I gave her my cell number so she could alert me if Mr. McMurtry went somewhere long enough for us to get in and out of the house.

"Call twice, let it ring once each time," I said. "That'll be the signal I should come right away."

"Why don't you just answer the phone?"

"Um, I don't want Mom or Dad to ask who's calling."

"Why not? Don't you want them to know you're coming here?"

"Not really, not unless you want me to answer all their questions about Piper, and the ponies, and your grandfather's cancer—"

She cut me off. "Okay, okay, I get it. Yeah, you're right. The code. That'll be our code. Keep this stuff to ourselves. No one needs to pry into our business. Ever."

It was only a tiny, little white lie, but it felt enormous. California was the last person I thought I'd keep a secret from, but I couldn't tell her how Mom felt about her family. It would hurt California, and embarrass me.

"I'm really sorry about today, Annie-girl. Sometimes I go a little out of my head, you know?"

That was the thing. I didn't know what it was like to be California any more than she knew what it was like to be Annie Stockton. But when we were together, none of that mattered, because that's when we were We.

ELEVEN

A note lay open on the kitchen counter.

Pumpkin

We'll be back from the lake at 6:00. Mom says please take the lobster bisque from the fridge and put it on low heat at 5:45.

See you soon.

Love,

Dad

It took a minute to sink in that Mom trusted me to do this without hovering. I checked the fridge, found the bisque, and set the alarm on my cell for five thirty. After a shower I let my hair loose and flipped the ends the way she liked, hoping clean shorts, a polo shirt, and a smearing of her beige makeup would distract from my sunburn.

At dinner I slid into my chair and smiled at both of them. Mom's mouth flickered a sign of approval. Everyone fell into an awkward silence. Dad studied the pink liquid in his bowl. Mom chewed tiny pieces of lobster. I swirled my spoon around and watched the cream run off.

"Annabel—"

I ignored her.

"I'm sorry. Annie." She wiggled in her chair like she was shaking off the fact that my name change still bothered her. "The clambake is tomorrow night. It would mean a lot if you came. We haven't been to the beach together as a family all summer. If you come, I'll buy you a new outfit to wear." She squeezed her napkin so tight it would take an hour to iron out the wrinkles.

I didn't want a new outfit, and I didn't want to go to the clambake. Since the panic attacks started, my social life had ceased to exist. While Jessica was going to boy-girl parties, I'd stayed home, avoiding crowds. Crowds made my throat feel like it was closing. So no, I did not want to go to the clambake.

But what if, instead of asking me to go to a clambake, what if Mom had announced she had cancer? What if she said it could come back, and there might be limited clambakes in our future? My stomach pitched. Her expression was so hopeful.

"I don't want a new outfit, but I'll go with you." The last word wasn't even out of my mouth before my throat tightened.

Dad patted my arm. "It'll be fine, Pumpkin. Once you take that first step, it's going to feel like old times." He dunked a chunk of French bread into his bisque. Mom smiled and stirred. I put my spoon down and stared at my bowl until dinner was over.

My mind reeled all night. I dreamed of showing up at school naked and getting stuck in a crowd of people laughing at me. By morning the neck of my T-shirt was damp and bunched, and my fingers didn't want to uncurl from the fabric. A fast hike through the woods with California would have worn down my nerves, but she was MIA. I hung around the orchard, hiding behind a tree, and waited. She never went to the river without me. Where was she? The gate creaked on the back side of the barn. I turned sharply and fled.

When I got home, a new sundress was spread out on my bed. White eyelet. Eyelet! Like what six-year-olds wear on Easter. Next to the dress was a pair of white sandals with shiny gold bumblebees in the middle. A piece of Mom's engraved stationery lay open with a note written in her perfect calligraphic script.

In case you change your mind about the new outfit
Love,
Mom

At five o'clock I met Mom and Dad at the car. No one said anything about my shorts and flip-flops. Nothing with actual words, anyway.

The sun inched its way toward the line of trees across the lake. Strings of white lights twinkled along the roof of the boathouse. Two dozen tiki torches rose from the sand around the edge of the small beach, and reflections from the flames spilled across the water like gold coins. Families I'd known my entire life gathered around tables and red-hot charcoal pits. Little kids ran from one side of the beach to the other, their hands clutching flame-spitting sparklers. So many people. I got stuck at the top of the stone steps, gripping the rail, fighting panic.

Dad put his hand on my back. "You look great, Pumpkin."

He led us to an empty table where the beach jutted out like a finger and set a cooler of clams down on the glass tabletop. I sank into the closest chair and picked the hairs at the nape of my neck. Each little prick gave one millisecond of relief from the looming panic. The familiar scent of lime and charcoal settled around me. This was a happy smell. This was normal.

Breathe in, breathe out.

The vise gripping my shoulders started to loosen.

"Vicky? Pumpkin? What would my two favorite girls like from the bar?" Dad winked at me. *You okay?*

I nodded and said, "Diet Coke and an aspirin, please."

He chuckled and turned to Mom.

"Plain tonic water with lime for me."

She emptied the contents of the picnic basket onto the table, lining up everything in some kind of specific order apparent only to her. Dad patted my shoulder and wandered off, greeting friends with smiles and handshakes. It was so easy for him—the whole social thing. So natural. I turned back to watch Mom arrange our food with the sinking realization she and I shared the same awkwardness.

She paused in her relentless organizing and frowned at me.

"What's wrong?"

"Shoulders. You're slouching."

Far in the distance, across the lake, up the side of the hill and through the trees, lights twinkled, white against dark green. Mr. McMurtry's house. Wherever she'd been, California must be home now. I unslouched my shoulders.

"Mom?"

"Hmmm?"

"Did Mr. McMurtry ever come to the clambake?"

She paused, and I immediately wanted to take the question back. "I assume he did, why?"

"Just curious."

Tommy's mom, Mrs. Radcliffe, called from across the beach. "Vicky? We're over here." She waved a jiggly arm sheathed in hot-pink chiffon. Mrs. Radcliffe's claim to fame was her extensive wardrobe of wild-colored muumuus and her knowledge of how to mix every drink in *The Bartender's Guide*. Mom's mouth curved up at the invitation. She turned to me.

"Want to go sit with the Radcliffes?"

"No, I'm good, thanks."

She looked back over to Mrs. Radcliffe and shook her head.

"You don't have to stay here and babysit me."

"I don't want to leave you alone," she mumbled.

"Mom, really, go. I'm totally fine alone. I don't want them to come over here."

She wasn't convinced.

"The Freedom Plan, remember? My decision doesn't mean you have to stay with me."

Mom watched Mrs. Radcliffe mixing something in a silver shaker. "Are you sure?"

"Positive. One hundred percent."

She still had her worried-about-Annabel vibe. "Tell Dad, okay?" She lifted the cooler of clams and headed off.

I turned my chair to face the water and slid down. All

around me glasses clinked, butter sizzled on hot coals, and strings of plastic American flags flapped in the breeze—all sounds that used to make me happy. Now they meant crowds. Panic attacks. I laced my fingers together in my lap, not sure what else to do with my hands. California's binky comment still stung, so I'd left my notebook at home and had nothing to doodle in. With any luck I'd get through the evening without being noticed.

"Annabel!"

Nope.

I still hadn't seen Tommy, but there he was, striding toward me, his face lit up like a Christmas tree, waving his whole arm in the air so everyone turned to stare.

"Hey, where've you been?"

The plastic chair disengaged from the backs of my sweaty thighs with a loud sucking noise when I stood up. Tommy gave me a one-armed hug. A strange girl had her hand clasped around his elbow. "This is a friend of mine, Sam. She's visiting from Savannah."

"Hi, Annabel," Sam-from-Savannah drawled. "That's such a lovely name."

I'd never heard anyone say my name with so many vowels in it. "Thanks, but I go by Annie now."

Sam-from-Savannah looped her arm through Tommy's and smiled. She was wearing baby-pink lip gloss. "Annie is just as sweet." Pure honey couldn't have flowed any thicker.

She tilted her head so wisps of pale hair fell over her eyes, then blew them away with a delicate puff, like she was kissing the air. Sam looked like a slightly older, Southern version of the city girls I'd had as friends, before the panic attacks. Before I got to spend my days on a farm like I'd always wanted. Before I understood what Dr. Clementi meant when he said you can't fit a square peg—*me*—into a round hole—*the wrong life*.

Sam had perfectly smooth, blond hair, feathered at the bottom, and matching lashes over turquoise eyes. Her crisp, white sundress and sandals were almost identical to the ones stuffed in the back of my closet, minus the bumblebees. Mom would love Sam-from-Savannah all the way to the end of her perfectly tanned feet and pampered, pink toenails.

"Thank you," I croaked.

Tommy touched my arm. "What have you been up to all summer?"

Sam watched me like a fat cat watches goldfish trapped in a cement pond.

"I've been busy. Really busy."

"You wanna sail together on Sunday?" he asked.

Sam shifted her shoulder so it edged between Tommy and me. "Yes, come sail with us, Annie. We can make room for you."

"That's okay," I said. "I've got somewhere to go."

"You always used to sail. Where are you going?" Tommy asked.

"Just somewhere." I shifted from one foot to the other.

Sam raised her eyebrows and smirked, forcing me to blurt out something really stupid. "I'm helping a friend with her ponies."

"Whose ponies?"

Tommy knew I'd never ridden a pony. He knew almost everything about me, except how much I'd always *wanted* to ride a pony. He didn't even know my secret dream of living on a farm, or that I was writing a story, or that stuffy lake people made me feel inferior. He didn't know I felt like a klutz when I took tennis and ballet lessons, and that I preferred a symphony of crickets over anything I could hear in the city. He had no idea I'd had panic attacks all year; that the panic attacks had scared away all my school friends, and I'd replaced them with someone who was nothing—*nothing*—like anyone he knew, and I'd rather go on ten hot pony searches with California than be stuck on that beach with him and Sam-from-Savannah for five minutes.

So, really, Tommy Radcliffe knew nothing about me. Nothing that mattered, anyway.

"No one you know. It's a friend who lives on a farm."

"A farm around here? You mean that crazy guy with the corn?"

I'd given away too much. Tommy could say something to his parents about me hanging around on McMurtry's farm. They would definitely say something to Mom.

"No, no, not anyone you know. I'm helping, um, no one around here. That's all." My whole entire body was on fire.

Sam did the tilted-head-because-I'm-so-cute thing and asked, "Are you okay, Annie—"

Tommy interrupted her. "Aren't you going to sail at all this summer?"

"Of course I'm going to sail, and play tennis, yeah, all summer. I've been so busy, you know, summer reading, all that summer homework—"

A flush from being caught in this weird trap crept up my neck. Sam smiled, but not a nice kind of smile. The kind that made me feel stupid.

"Tommy, I'm going over there." She motioned toward the Radcliffes' table with a jerk of her head. "Clearly your friend isn't interested in anything we have to offer. So nice to meet you, Annabel-slash-Annie." She flipped her hair and pranced away across the sand.

Tommy's face fell. He looked from me to Sam's retreating back like he couldn't pick which side of the war to fight on.

"Tommy, I'm—"

"I have to—" He sidestepped in Sam's direction.

Past Tommy, across the lake, the lights from California's house still twinkled, warm and welcoming. I thought about the fight she and I had the day before, and how it got fixed so easily because we had that kind of friendship. A real one.

I didn't belong on this beach with these people anymore.

"I'm sorry, Tommy."

He turned away to follow Sam, and one more string fell away from its grip around my neck.

TWELVE

At 7:55 the next morning, California used the code to summon me. I dressed in thirty seconds and raced downstairs. Mom and Dad were having coffee on the deck. I slid the door open and stuck my head outside.

"Hey, I'm leaving," I said, trying to shut it before they asked any questions.

"Where are you off to already?" Mom asked.

"Pumpkin?"

My mind went blank until I saw the firefly jar sitting on the edge of the deck, the one I'd hidden the cloth in the day I'd met California.

"Going to see if I can find more raspberries." I looked right at Mom and lied. "Maybe we can make jam." That one slipped out way too easily.

"Jam?" Her joy at the idea of us making jam together was almost worse than if she'd been mad.

"This early?" Dad asked.

"It's supposed to be in the nineties later."

"Do you have a basket to carry them in?" Mom started to get up, which meant a lengthy search for the perfect basket, and an inquisition. "You need the right kind—"

"I'm good, already have it. Bye, see you later!"

I quickly closed the door and left her standing at the edge of the deck, coffee cup in hand, mouth open in silent protest. Dad's hand gripped the edge of her bathrobe, holding her back.

California was waiting for me in the orchard, pacing the fence line. "Sorry to use the code for something else, but I needed you to come fast."

"What do you mean? Is your grandfather still home?"

"He left for Saratoga-something-or-other. We'll investigate inside later. This is too important to wait. Follow me."

She took off running, with me right behind her. At the bottom of the hill, we ducked into the woods near a lone dogwood and raced down the path our own feet had made. The oak came into view, and I jerked to a stop. A thick bunch of pine boughs were propped against one side of the trunk like half a tepee.

"What's that?"

"Come see."

California crawled underneath. Inside, a large, gray dog's body stretched over a ratty blanket stained with dried blood and pus. One leg, right above a back paw, was mangled.

"What happened?"

California kissed the top of the dog's head and stroked the ruff of black and white hairs around his neck. "He hobbled up the hill yesterday dragging an animal trap behind him. Luckily, I saw him before Grandfather did—he would have shot him."

The dog was so still, if he hadn't blinked I would have taken him for dead.

"How'd you get him down here?"

"Wheelbarrow. Took me almost two hours. I had to wrench the trap off him too. Bet he weighs more than you, even thin as he is. Feel his ribs."

I opened my fingers and buried them in his hair, one in between each rib. It was a dog—a beautiful, mostly alive dog. My hand moved to his hip, to his thigh, and down toward his paw. The closer I got to the wound, the hotter his skin. "He has an infection."

"I know. He's probably going to die, but at least he'll know someone loved him."

She rubbed her cheek along the top of his head. It wasn't like California to give up so easily.

"Maybe he doesn't have to die. Maybe we can help him."

She rolled her fingertip in a circle around his ear. "I've thought about it all night. We don't have medicine. And even if we found a vet to fix him, who would pay for it? There's only so much paying-for-things Grandfather's going to do. Saving an old dog isn't on the list."

My whole life I'd wanted a dog, one that would lie on my bed at night and stay by my side through thick and thin. I'd begged and pleaded. I'd even gotten Dad on my side this year and used my panic attacks to try to persuade Mom we could get a service dog, like our neighbor Mrs. James, who got a golden retriever because of her seizures. Mom's answer never wavered. There would be no dog hair on the furniture, no trekking down the sidewalk, plastic bag in hand, picking up "waste." In other words, there would be no dog in my life as long as I lived with her.

Until now. And right that second, there wasn't anything I wanted more in the world than to nurse that dog back to health.

"I can search the internet and bring supplies from home. We've got more medical stuff than a drugstore. We can help him. I know we can!"

California got a curious expression, then whispered in the dog's ear. After a few seconds, he shifted his shoulder and licked her fingers.

"Okay," she said. "It's worth a try."

✴✴✴✴✴✴✴✴✴✴✴✴✴✴✴✴✴✴✴✴✴✴✴✴

An hour later my fingers clicked the keyboard: *dog infected wound*. My foot tapped under Dad's desk. "Come on, Google."

A dog—barely alive, so beautiful, and I might be able to save him.

The computer screen changed, and a photo of a brown, curly-haired dog appeared. Its leg was bandaged, and a white-coated vet stood by with a smile on her face that promised, *This dog will live*. I wanted to do what that vet had done. I wanted to save the dog. I zoomed in on the image and studied the way the bandage was wrapped, then hit Print. The article said: Clean with warm, soapy water, rinse, pat dry, and get antibiotics from your vet. God save that poor creature down by the river, because all he was getting was me.

There were four prescription bottles in the medicine cabinet. I ran back to the computer and typed fast. The first three were useless. The fourth was an antibiotic for humans with Dad's name on the label. My fingers tapped the keys again: *Amoxicillin for dogs?*

Yes!

Ripping the picture from the printer, I put the other bottles back and raced through the house like my feet were on fire, gathering supplies before Mom and Dad came back. Within minutes, my backpack was stuffed with towels, scissors, the ice pack from the freezer, hydrogen peroxide, first-aid ointment, tweezers, cotton balls, a plastic bowl, a chunk of leftover steak, the seven antibiotics left in the bottle, and two granola bars.

That backpack might as well have been loaded with hot bricks instead of towels and medicine. When I reached the lone dogwood at the edge of the woods, I turned gratefully into the shade of our homemade trailhead. That's what California told me it was called. A trailhead. One word, no capital letters.

She was still sitting under the pine boughs when I got back. The dog was so quiet I stopped short, afraid he'd died while I'd been searching for ways to save him. His sides rose and fell. He was alive. California had been crying, the flesh underneath her eyes puffed and pinky gray. I cringed at the sight of her mourning over that dog like he was her very own Romeo, dying in her arms.

I piled the stolen supplies in the dirt. "I got stuff—antibiotics, hydrogen peroxide, all kinds of stuff."

She barely acknowledged me. "Annie, he can't die."

"I know. We'll fix him. Let's start with getting him hydrated."

The poor dog could barely lift his head to drink the water I got from the river, so I cupped my hands and let him lap it with his tongue.

"That's a good boy," I said. "Did you name him?"

"Not until you told me you could save him. It would've been bad luck. You can save him, right?"

Oh, God, I hope so.

"I named him Field. That's where I found him, and that's the next part of Piper's song. 'Peaches and Cream and fields of green,' remember? I found him in her fields of green."

I smiled at her logic. "Maybe naming him Field will bring us good luck."

"He's going to need more than luck. That's a mangled mess."

"First up is to wash those cuts. Hold him steady, 'kay?"

I picked up the scissors and began snipping away the hair around the ugly, red wounds. Every time I dribbled peroxide on raw flesh, Field curled his three good legs and whimpered. No sign of biting. Everything was going great until California decided to sing that awful song to him. She belted it so loud the birds flew away. I stuffed cotton in my ears when she wasn't looking.

"'PeachesandCreamandfieldsofgreenmemoriesfromlong-ago'"—*inhale*—"'Iweepforyouwithbrokenheart'"—*sniffle*—"'underthewillowunderthewillow.'"

I tried to drown out the sour notes by thinking of the beautiful music Mom and I played together, but all I heard was the harshness of California's voice. Field shivered—and not because of what I was doing to his leg. I peered closer, cutting pus-crusted hair from around the wound. In some places the flesh was so ragged I had to use tweezers to pick out the pieces of dried leaves and dirt. He must have dragged that trap for miles.

California nudged me. I pulled a cotton ball out of one ear. "What?"

"Why do you have cotton in your ears?"

I tugged at a bloody pine needle, dropped it onto a piece of gauze, and held it out. "Because I need to concentrate on this, not your singing."

She scowled but kept her mouth shut. I dug back to work. Kneeling under those pine boughs, working my way through every detail of cleaning Field's wound, a new and exciting idea came to life. Maybe I could be like that vet in the picture. Maybe I didn't have to be a professor, like I'd always assumed. Maybe I could choose my own career. I could be a writer if I wanted. Or a journalist who wrote for veterinary magazines. There were so many possibilities.

When I was done, I sat back and admired my work. The edges of the wounds looked like they'd been professionally trimmed. The two deepest gashes were closed with tape, and the rest was clean and smeared with bacteria-killing ointment.

"Only thing left are the antibiotics, but I'm not sure he'll eat them."

"Let me see that bottle." California shook out a chalky pill and broke it in half. Holding Field's mouth open, she dropped each piece on the back of his tongue and jammed her finger inside, pushing them down his throat, then held his mouth closed until he swallowed. "That's how we do it with calves."

We tucked the rags under the bad leg and pulled the soiled blanket out. "Tomorrow we should bring clean sheets.

This blanket is nasty, and the flies are going to be horrible," I said.

"We have shoofly plants near the woodpile. I can chop up the roots and mix them with milk to dab around the wound. That keeps the flies away. I'll bring some later. Grandfather's going to be home soon. We'd better get back. He's bringing me a baby chicken."

"For what?"

"I thought about what you said, about there being other things to make it like it was when Piper was growing up. She had chickens, so I told him I wanted one for a pet. I'm gonna build a chicken coop, like she had when she was a kid."

A baby chick—I'd finally get to hold a baby chick in my hands.

We said good-bye to Field and walked single file out of the woods, up the hill, and through the orchard, turning together toward the paddock. Gravel crunched in the driveway. Blue metal flashed on the other side of the barn. California'd seen it, too. We dodged behind a tree near the fence. Dad's Volvo turned out of the driveway.

"Oh, no!"

"What?"

I pointed at the car. "That was my dad. Why was he here?"

California stared at the Volvo as it crested the hill and dropped out of sight.

"I thought you told me they didn't know you were coming

here. Why would he be here? What was he trying to find out?"

Before I could gather my thoughts, someone else spoke. Someone watching us from the paddock, his voice low and firm.

"Catherine?"

We both turned, and I inhaled sharply. On the other side of the fence stood Mr. McMurtry, holding a red chicken in his arms.

THIRTEEN

With a jerk of his chin, Mr. McMurtry told us to follow him. I whispered urgently to California that I had to go home before Dad said anything to Mom, but she barreled past, her chin stuck out and her fingers clenched around my sleeve. We traipsed across the driveway, past a square patch of dug-up earth, home to a jumble of green things and blossoms that smelled like peppermint and sage. Mr. McMurtry stopped to shove the squawking chicken into a crate near the back steps, then held open a screen door and waved us inside.

The shock of seeing Dad drive away, and coming

face-to-face with Mr. McMurtry, disappeared as soon as I stepped into the kitchen, if that's what you'd call it. Except for missing a bed, the brick-floored space looked like all living happened in that one room. At the far end, a broom and hoe leaned against a stone fireplace. Old newspapers spilled out of baskets. A floral wing chair sagged under the weight of encyclopedias. A jug of Pepto-Bismol sat in the middle of a narrow wooden table, along with packages of paper plates and unopened mail. Toothbrushes in a jar and a Bible were propped on the windowsill over the sink. Every nook and cranny was crammed with bottles, mixing bowls, a vacuum cleaner, toilet paper, curtain rods—the mess went on and on.

But the most obvious thing in that room—the one you couldn't see—was a heavy sadness hanging thick, like a wet blanket. It was the saddest room I'd ever been in.

California swung past the refrigerator and swiped a piece of paper off the front, suspiciously similar to one of Mom's schedules. She plunked down in the nearest chair and stuffed it out of sight. Mr. McMurtry watched her, then cleared another chair of newspapers and socks for me. I perched on the edge, twisting a strand of hair around my fingers. California thrust her chin to her fist and stared at the table. Mr. McMurtry shuffled between the sink, the stove, and the fridge.

He picked up a copper colander and pulled out a hammer, a container of nails, and a plastic bag of dried leaves and withered, yellow buds. A teakettle whistled, and he dumped the leaves into a sieve and trickled boiling water over them into a pitcher. When the pitcher was full, he put a plate over the top and let it sit while he sliced a lemon. After swirling the pitcher a few times, he set it on the table next to the lemons and a sugar bowl, and gave each of us a glass of ice with a sprig of mint and a spoon.

"Chamomile and mint. Good for the nerves."

Sweat trickled along the edge of my hairline. "Thank you."

Mr. McMurtry tapped his heels together and nodded. "Catherine, would you offer your guest some of the oatmeal cookies you made?"

She swirled her tea and studied the way the mint bobbed below the surface. Mr. McMurtry's eyes sank at the corners. His cheekbones rose sharply above a hollow face, and when he skirted a glance and saw me watching him, he turned away. California got up and took two cookies from a glass jar, sliding one across the table to me. I held a paper towel underneath mine and pretended to nibble the edge. She didn't bother pretending anything; she spun her cookie in circles on the table while Mr. McMurtry fussed with something by the stove.

"Catherine is an excellent cook, Annabel."

She smacked the swirling cookie flat. "Her name is *Annie*, not Annabel."

Mr. McMurtry poured coffee from a carafe and sat down between us. "Annie, then." He dipped his head toward the mug so hair fell over his eyes. I was sorry California had made an issue of my name. It didn't matter enough to make everyone feel more uncomfortable. It was going to take a whole lot of happy tea to lift the spirits in that room.

Whenever I took a sip, I stole a peek at him over the top of my glass. He didn't seem too bad for someone who'd had cancer. His skin was rough, with jagged crevices running down the side of his cheeks, his arms muscled and tan. He rested his elbows on the table and wrapped enormous hands around his mug.

"Catherine."

She barely lifted her eyes from her glass.

"Don't worry," he said. His nose twitched, and he went back to his coffee.

Don't worry about what?

California glanced quickly at me. The weight in the room slowly shifted. She took her first taste of tea. Mr. McMurtry sipped his coffee. I put my mouth against the cold glass and inhaled the spicy scent of fresh-cut peppermint. California poured sugar in her drink, stirred, and sipped.

"You're supposed to put the sugar in while the tea is still hot, remember?" she said quietly.

"That's only if you want sweet tea. Some people don't like it sweet."

"Oh, right."

She got up, scraping her chair loudly on the brick floor, and brought three more cookies from the jar—another for each of us, and one for her grandfather.

"Is it a Rhode Island Red?"

Mr. McMurtry nodded. "There are three others," he said. "There's a Silver Spitzhauben chick, and two—"

"You brought me a Silver Spitzhauben?"

"Yes, a Silver chick, and two white Leghorns for laying."

California hit both hands to her chest and launched out of the chair. "A Silver Spitzhauben? I've never had a Silver before. Annie, Silver Spitzhaubens are one of the most beautiful chickens in the whole world!"

Mr. McMurtry's beard moved, and the corners of his eyes dropped farther. "You girls better get to work building a coop. Lumber and chicken wire are by the barn. I'll be out to help."

"Annie, come on. We got a Silver!" California bolted from the table and threw the screen door open so it slammed against the house. I picked up my glass and napkin, but Mr. McMurtry put his hand on my arm.

"You go with Catherine. I'll clean this up and come out to help in a few minutes."

I started toward the door but stopped short. They were wrong, all those people who whispered about him being crazy. They were wrong. He wasn't crazy. He wasn't evil. He was sad. The only thing he was hiding was the pain engraved on his face.

I turned back and said clearly, so he knew I meant it, "Thank you, Mr. McMurtry. I think California is really happy about the chickens."

California and her grandfather faced off during the coop-building episode. We'd already pulled the chicken wire and lumber over by the kitchen door when he came outside to help.

"Matilda will eat the chickens if the coop is next to the barn, Grandfather. You know that."

"I do, which is why I've been trying to get rid of that snake, but you keep bringing it back."

"Even if Matilda was gone, there'd be another snake. We need the coop near the house."

"Chicken coops smell."

"I know that. Back home Piper and I are in charge of the chickens and the cows, and they both smell."

Mr. McMurtry winced. "Build it wherever you want, but I expect it to stay immaculate."

California waited until he disappeared around the side of the house. "Works every time. I say Piper's name, and he gives up."

"Maybe you should be nicer to him."

"Why?"

"Because he's trying to be nice, and because he had cancer."

Mr. McMurtry came back with a box of supplies. "Where do you want these?"

"Over here, Grandfather, by the door, please," she answered, all sugary-sweet.

Mr. McMurtry deposited the box on the ground. "Annabel,

I told your father you would be home before six."

"Annie!" California scolded.

"Annie, then."

I wanted to tell him it didn't matter what he called me, and I wanted to ask why Dad had been there, but he was already walking away. He came back with two long wooden poles attached to curved paddles. California walked off three paces from the side of the house and slammed the paddles into the earth. She twisted and pushed and jiggled them back and forth, pulled out half a scoop of dirt, dumped it to the side, and went back for more.

"This is called a posthole digger."

She was as natural a hole digger as she was a swimmer, a raspberry picker, an apple tree climber, a snake handler—an all-around farm girl. She was everything I wanted to be.

"We're going to make four holes for the posts. We'll tack the chicken wire to them and have a shelter against the house. Oh, and a gate, I'm sure Grandfather got a gate. If not, we'll make one. I know how. Have you ever had real, farm-fresh eggs, right out of the nest?"

Slam, twist, pull, dump.

"You've probably never seen how yellow they are."

Slam, twist, pull, dump.

"You've only had store-bought eggs, right? Well, let me tell you, the difference is like nothing you've ever tasted."

Slam, twist, pull, dump.

"I bet if I made that lemon pie with these eggs, it'd be so

yellow you'd have to put on sunglasses."

California rambled on, digging, twisting, and dumping, digging, twisting, and dumping until late afternoon when we had a slightly crooked, six-by-eight-foot coop filled with sweet-smelling straw.

Mr. McMurtry brought a pitcher of ice water, two plastic cups, and more cookies in a napkin. California gulped her water so loud Mom could probably hear her a mile away. When she was done and ready to defend the special baby chick, she pushed her knuckles into her hips and braced her legs.

"The Silver isn't going to like being cooped up, Grandfather. They like to wander and roost in trees. She might get depressed."

"These are your chickens. You care for them and give me fresh eggs for breakfast. But if I step in chicken droppings one time, they'll be gone. Understood?"

She stopped ranting. "Does that mean you're going to eat breakfast with me from now on?"

Mr. McMurtry pointed to the ground. "Chicken droppings."

She smiled and waved her finger. "You won't even know they are here, except when I make you the best omelets you've ever eaten. Promise."

The Rhode Island Red went in first. She was short and fat, with beady, threatening eyes. California tossed a handful of cracked corn on the ground. The hen pecked, then deposited a load of black-and-white stuff behind her and burrowed into the straw.

Next came the two white hens, knee-high, with elegant tails fanning out behind them. They jerked their heads forward and back when they walked. After pecking the corn, they pooped, drank some water, and settled side by side in the straw.

Finally, Mr. McMurtry brought a cardboard box from the side of the house.

Tap-tap-tap.

California reached out with quivering hands. "The Silver?"

He nodded. When she lifted the lid and said "Oooohhhhh," Mr. McMurtry's eyes sank again—like the happier she got, the more he hurt. She reached inside and brought out the tiny chick cupped in her hands.

"My very own Silver. Isn't she beautiful, Annie?"

It wasn't beautiful. It looked diseased and was uglier than California's epiglottis. Part of her was white, part black, part fuzz, part feather, with black eyes that blinked nonstop and a puff of something like a mistake sprouting from the top of her head. California cradled it against her cheek.

"Let's name her Lacy, because when all her feathers come in, she'll look like she has black lace over a white body."

So there was hope for the poor creature.

"Catherine." Mr. McMurtry pointed toward the coop.

The Rhode Island Red was off her nest, scouting around

for food. In the straw where she'd been sitting was one perfect café au lait–colored egg. California's face lit up. She opened the new gate, crept past the chickens, and gently lifted the egg off the straw. When she was back out, she wrapped it in a paper towel and held it out to me, her face beaming.

"Piper's meeting us next week. I really should save this for her. But I want you to have it, Annie. It's a gift. My very first East Coast egg for my very first East Coast friend."

FOURTEEN

When I stepped into the kitchen at ten minutes before six, hiding that tawny first egg in a handkerchief behind my back, my stomach knotted. Why had Dad been at the farm? Had he told Mom about California? Was she going to be ballistic?

Instead, it was like entering an alternate universe. Mom and Dad stood side by side, chopping vegetables on the butcher-block island. Dad wore a red-and-white-striped apron around his waist. A slightly off-center, starched chef hat perched on Mom's head. Dad dumped a handful of red and yellow peppers into a bowl.

"Hey, Pumpkin, how was your day?"

"Fine."

Their knives chopped in unison. Chop-chop-chop. They chopped mushrooms, onions, and black olives, tossing them into the same bowl. *The same bowl.* Mom never mixed things in the same bowl.

"What's all that?"

Mom straightened her chef hat and blushed. "We're making homemade pizza."

"We flipped a coin. She wears the hat, and I wear the apron."

Mom giggled and sliced into a beautiful, red tomato. We never ate pizza at home. Pizza was for Casual Night Out. Emphasis on *out.* And even then we couldn't simply go eat pizza. It had to be a cultural experience, where we talked about things like how the early Greeks made *plantkuntos* as an edible plate for stews that evolved into pizza crust.

The only time I'd eaten pizza at home was when Mom was away. Dad came in with a wicked smile and made me pinky-swear I would never tell. We walked three blocks in the snow to the local pizza parlor and spent half an hour deciding on a pie to bring home. We put garbage bags over the couch and on the floor, so if anything dripped Mom would never know, and sat with our feet propped on the coffee table—barbarian style—the pizza box between us, dripping sauce all over our clothes, drinking Stewart's birch beer, and laughing at *My Cousin Vinny.* That was the only time, and she still didn't know.

Mom stuck her head in the pantry, and Dad whispered out the side of his mouth, "She's doing this for you. Just go with it."

"Why were you at Mr. McMurtry's today?" I whispered back.

She pulled her head out of the pantry. "What was that?"

"Um, do I have time for a shower?"

"Hurry, I heard thunder a minute ago." I disappeared before the don't-shower-during-a-thunderstorm debate started.

I lay the egg on top of crumpled tissues inside a shoe box and hid it behind my suitcase in the very back of my closet. After a hot shower, I followed the aroma of tomatoes and basil through the kitchen to the dining room. The table was bare.

"We're in here."

I peered around the corner into the living room. Mom and Dad sat shoulder to shoulder on the love seat. Mom smoothed a red-and-white-checkered cloth on the coffee table. In the center, on top of a round, silver tray, was a magnificent, steaming pizza pie, loaded with veggies and cheese and sauce on a perfectly browned crust. Next to the pizza was a stack of white Chinet paper plates—paper plates!

"Um . . . have you guys been drinking the funny Kool-Aid?"

"Come sit. Let's eat," Dad said.

"Is everything okay?"

Mom lifted a shiny pizza-cutting wheel and the silver cake server from the table. "Of course. We thought you might like something a little less . . . well, a little more . . . um. Richard, would you like to cut it?" She handed him the utensils and spread two peach-colored linen napkins across her lap.

She'd really made pizza. We were actually going to eat it in the living room. This was totally weird. But I didn't say that. I said, "This looks great!"

I ate the pizza with my hands like we did at school. Mom never said a word. She couldn't, anyway, because Dad never stopped yakking.

"Did you know I spent a summer in Italy after my sophomore year in college? It was right before I met your mom, and there was this girl I was trying to impress. . . ."

He rattled on about the girl's uncle teaching him to toss the dough and how the girl laughed like a hyena when he dropped it on the floor. "Good thing I heard that girl's awful laugh or I might never have met your mom."

Mom blushed and dabbed at her mouth with a napkin, frowning at the red stain—one more thing for her to wash and iron. I already knew from the ironing lessons she'd made me endure that linen is next to impossible.

"Mom, have you ever thought of using paper napkins?" Her body stiffened. "I mean, so you don't have to spend all summer ironing."

She settled back against the love seat and studied Grandmother Stockton's mirror across the room like she always did when she had a manners-related decision to make. After a moment she said, "No, no, I never did consider that."

"I don't mind paper napkins, Vic."

"Well, I don't mind ironing," she said, sprinkling Parmesan over her pizza with a tiny silver salt spoon. "And neither did your mother."

Dad reached over and patted the top of her hand. "You don't have to do everything the way she did. We love you just the way you are."

Mom stopped sprinkling. "Sometimes you say things that make it sound like I come up short in your mind. I can't help it if my upbringing didn't come with the perks yours did."

"You don't need perks, babe. You're perfect. And my mother didn't have the smarts you do, so you're one up on her."

The corners of Mom's mouth curved up. She might even have been blushing. Dad and I relaxed, and we all went back to our pizza.

After we did the dishes and moved the furniture back the way it was supposed to be, the three of us watched *Forrest Gump*. It was Mom and Dad's favorite movie, the good old standby. Dad and I called, "Ruuuun, Forrest, ruuuun," and giggled when Forrest said, "Jenneaaa." Mom grabbed the box of tissues when Forrest watched cartoons with his little boy. And when it was over, I felt so warm and fuzzy I hugged them both before going upstairs to write a new chapter about Scout and Liberty. It was a great feeling.

FIFTEEN

T he next morning my phone rang twice, this time a little after eight. California and I had already made plans to meet by the river after noon, so this meant Mr. McMurtry must be going somewhere long enough for us to do a search in the house first. I tiptoed quietly past Mom and Dad's room, and left a note on the counter.

In search of raspberries. Back later. A.

Another lie. Someday, I promised myself, I'd make up for the lies and bring home a huge bucket of raspberries, and I'd stand in the kitchen with Mom all day and make jam until we were swimming in it.

California met me on the road, bouncing in the air like Tigger when she saw me coming.

"Hurry. I already fed Field, so we can search the other places. I have a good feeling about today. We're going to find something new, I just know it!"

We ran past the orchard, climbed the fence into the paddock, and dodged into the barn at the same time a car passed on the road and honked. Mom and Dad hadn't had time to get up and drive a mile, so I pushed the nagging worry out of my head and followed California. She gave me a crude, hand-drawn map.

"Before we go in the house, let's cover this whole barn, top to bottom. You take this side—check the stalls, feel around for loose floorboards, check the feed room, behind those barrels of oats, and search the space underneath the stairs. Check for footprints in the dirt, poke around in every corner. I'm searching the carriage room."

We separated, and I startled at a shadow along the edge of the floor. "Wait!"

California turned back.

"What about Matilda? Where is she?"

"I don't know, but if you come across her, tell her you're sorry for interrupting her nap and move on. She's a black snake. Not poisonous. Not aggressive. Not interested in anything but finding mice and staying out of the heat."

My feet were lodged into the floor.

"Annie, are you really going to let a stupid old black snake hold us up?"

My mind wound itself up and spun so fast I could barely keep up. *Scout.* What would she do? My fictitious Scout, who was a little wild and a lot brave. She wouldn't let anything hold her back, just like California wasn't going to let anything keep her from bringing her mother home.

"I'm okay," I said. This was my chance to prove I could be like Scout, not just in the Story Notebook but in real life. I picked a place on the map to start and moved on.

Half an hour later I'd scoured every inch of space she'd assigned me. Only thing I found were dirty mousetraps, a couple of pieces of mildewed leather, and more cobwebs than I ever imagined could be in the entire state of New York. She hadn't found anything, either.

"Should we try the attic and his bedroom?" I asked.

"We probably should have started there. Now I'm scared he'll come back, and we'll be stuck in the attic until a search-and-rescue team comes looking."

"How many times did you go through that trunk upstairs?"

"Only twice, why?"

"If you were in a hurry, you could have missed something. Maybe we should check again."

She looked over to the driveway. "Like now?"

"Yeah, why not? Your grandfather's still gone, but if he comes back, it'll be easier to get out from up there before he catches us."

We ran up the stairs to the secret room. She grabbed the key out of the drawer, and the trunk lid popped open, revealing the box of ribbons and stacks of photos.

"Get the ribbons first," I said. "Maybe there's something written on the back of one you didn't notice before."

California grabbed the box, but when she lifted it up, the top popped off. A long, tricolor ribbon fell out. The end of the blue streamer was wedged between two pieces of wood. She tugged at it gently.

"It's caught on something. I'm scared I'm going to rip it," she said, squeezing her fingers into a narrow gap. The shelf shifted. "Hey, there's a whole other compartment underneath here."

Snatching the photographs from the other side of the trunk, she tossed them onto the floor. The wooden partition in the middle of the shelf had a hole in it, like a handle. With a few hefty tugs, she pulled it out. Underneath, a hidden cavity was filled with tennis trophies, fat manila envelopes, plastic bags full of loose photographs, all kinds of things that qualified as treasure box worthy. On the very bottom lay a brown leather satchel with the initials MKM embossed on the front. She held this up by a strap and touched the letters.

"Margaret Kathryn McMurtry. Piper has an old school shirt in her closet with these same letters embroidered on it. This was her satchel. You were right, Annie—he did save everything!"

A moth landed on the lightbulb hanging from the ceiling and made it flicker. Out in the carriage house, a family of barn swallows argued in high-pitched chirps. California and

I stood side by side, silent. She used her bare toe to shuffle some of the papers around on the floor.

"Now what do we do?" I finally asked.

"I—I guess we start going through it. Come on, let's take it to the river. Maybe we'll find something else totally new that could make her come home, like you said."

I carefully filled the satchel with papers and plastic bags, but California stopped me. "He might come back up here while we're gone and check the trunk. We don't want him to see things are missing."

"Right, of course."

After putting half the items back, California plumped the rest up so it wasn't as noticeable at a glance that some were missing. On our way out of the barn, the old Buick careened into the driveway. I tossed the satchel through the carriage house door behind me so Mr. McMurtry wouldn't see it.

"Catherine, we're late. Come get in the car."

"Late?"

"Your mother, we promised we would Skype today. We've got a room reserved at the library for you. Come, now."

"What time is it?"

"Past time. She's probably in a panic."

"Grandfather, Piper doesn't pani—"

Mr. McMurtry threw his hands up and motioned for her to get in the car. "My apologies, Annabel. We have to hurry."

California turned to me and flung her hand in the direction

of my house. "The satchel," she whispered urgently. "Take it."

Then they were gone, gravel spewing from under the tires as Mr. McMurtry did a U-turn in the driveway and sped off. There was nothing left but silence, the satchel, and me, standing alone in the chaos of someone else's life.

SIXTEEN

It was lunchtime when I walked slowly up our steep driveway. So much had happened over the morning, the only
thing on my mind was getting food and a nap. If I waltzed
into the house with the satchel slung over my shoulder, there
would be an interrogation, so I hid it under the deck with a
plan to sneak it to my room when Mom and Dad left for the
beach. That was my intention, anyway. Mom and Dad had
other ideas.

"Hey, Pumpkin, we were worried you wouldn't make it in
time."

I stopped short. Mom was wearing a skirt. Dad had on

slacks and a sport coat. A memory nibbled at my mind.

"In time for what?"

"We've got matinee tickets for *Twelfth Night* in Glens Falls. Did you forget?"

"*Twelfth Night*?" My mind had turned to mush.

Dad pulled the corner of his coat up over half his face like a mask and flailed his arm in the air. "Yes. Love: the ultimate act of deception, mixed with a bit of British humor."

"Deception?"

"Annie, Shakespeare, *Twelfth Night*. It's one of your favorites," Mom said.

My shoulders sank so far I thought my T-shirt might slip off. "Shakespeare, oh, right. Do you already have a ticket for me? I really want to take a nap."

Dad's face went blank, and Mom's sagged. My own deception was about to get me into real trouble. I brightened up quickly.

"Oh, *Twelfth Night*! Yeah, okay, yeah, sorry, I thought you meant— Never mind. What should I wear? I'll hurry."

My punishment was Mom following me upstairs, alert and excited that I'd asked her advice on what to wear. She pursed her lips when I put my foot down at the white eyelet sundress. A good compromise, in my opinion, was my short jean skirt and sandals. Not the bumblebee ones. Regular, teenager sandals.

I barely remember the play, or the "après-theater" supper as Mom called it, except for when my head bobbed dangerously close to my plate of calamari, and Dad stuck his finger in my ear to keep me awake. By the time we got home, I was comatose in the backseat.

"Pumpkin, you're too old for me to carry you up to bed. You've got to walk yourself."

Stumbling up the stairs, I fell asleep on top of my covers, still wearing my skirt and sandals.

At least once every summer a thunderstorm knocks out our power. It happened a few hours after we all went to bed. Raindrops pelted against the window screen and broke into a mist, soaking me and my pillow. I woke with a start, gasping for air and feeling like something was very wrong. There should have been fresh, dry towels on my bathroom shelf, but they weren't there. They were down by the river, tucked underneath Field's leg. He must be soaked. I changed into dry pajamas, fumbled back to bed, and reached over to shut the window. Water ran in a steady stream down the gutters outside, soaking the ground. The entire earth was going to turn to mud.

The entire earth.

Under the deck.

The satchel!

I leaped across my room and flew down the stairs two at a time, my footsteps muffled by rain pounding the roof. *Ohnoohnoohnoohno—please let it be okay.*

The couch was gone to be recovered, and Mom had

scattered different chairs around the room until it came back. I knocked into one and stubbed my toe. The second one I hit full force. We both crashed to the floor. I waited, listening. When I was sure no one had heard, I got up, raced outside, slogged through the mud under the deck, and pulled the satchel out. It was too late. A slick layer of brown goop coated the whole thing. Dirty water seeped all over the front of me. I'd ruined the papers before I'd even seen them. Stepping carefully across the deck, I went back inside and closed the sliding door behind me. The sound of water falling from my clothes splashed on the floor. Drip. Drip. Drip.

A yellow light bobbed in the hallway, turned the corner, and blinded me.

"Pumpkin? What are you doing down here? You're soaked. Why were you outside, and what's that?"

I gripped the satchel tighter. "Dad . . ."

"What's going on?" His voice had an unfamiliar edge.

"Dad—I, . . . can you . . . I need—"

A new wave of water spread across my belly. Hot tears trickled down my cheeks. "It's California's stuff. I left it outside, and it's soaked. It's all her mother's personal papers and photos. I had to go get it. What do I do?"

He watched me for a second and wiped a hand across his face.

"Dad?"

"I don't know what to tell you. This is getting out of hand."

"What? Dad, no—can you at least help me get back to my

room? I can't see anything."

The beam moved away, and he reached for me. "Come on."

I tiptoed toward him, my arms crossed over the satchel, over my heart. "I'm sorry. I didn't mean to make such a mess."

He shone the light in front so I could see where I was going. We turned the corner on the landing, and Mom's silhouette loomed large and dark at the top of the stairs.

"Richard?"

Dad flipped the flashlight away from me and shone it at her. She raised a hand to shield her eyes.

"Richard, you took the flashlight. I can't see. Is everything okay?"

One beat. Two beats. Dad didn't say anything.

"Annie?"

"It's me. And Dad."

"What are you doing down there? It's pitch-black. Do you have your flashlight?"

"No."

"What were you doing? Richard, what's going on?"

Dad nudged me from behind like he was saying, *"This is your moment, Pumpkin. Go for it!"* Why was he picking this exact moment to stop interfering?

"It was me. I got confused. Everything's so dark," I said.

"Why were you downstairs?"

She stepped onto the first stair. I hugged the satchel closer. "I, um, I was trying to find the fuse box. The lights are out."

"The lights won't come back on from flipping the fuse in a storm. Everyone's electricity is out." She blocked the light with her hand. "Do you even know where the fuse box is?"

"No."

"Richard, you should show her tomorrow."

Dad shifted behind me. "Sure, we can do that. Here, Pumpkin, let me through so I can help Mom back to bed."

He handed me the flashlight, pushed past, and led Mom away, leaving me alone on the stairs.

At the first hint of light I headed for the laundry room with my wet clothes rolled up inside a T-shirt. Dad was on his hands and knees by the door, rubbing a towel on the hardwood floor. Rain still hummed along the roof.

"Hi, Dad."

He kept mopping and said, "Shhhh. Mom's still sleeping."

I squeezed the bundle of muddy clothes and took a step toward the laundry room.

"Wait one second," he whispered. He motioned for me to sit on the sofa. "We need to talk."

"You already know what happened."

"You lied to Mom, Annie. That's not a good way to handle your problems. I don't think you even blinked an eye."

"Oh."

"Yeah, oh. Not good. Are there other things you've been lying about?"

"Nothing, I promise. I didn't know what to say."

"However beautiful the strategy, you should occasionally look at the results."

"Huh?"

"Winston Churchill. It means, pay attention to how you handle your affairs, because going down the wrong path can bring unpleasant results."

"Oh."

"One lie leads to another, and everything has to be covered up. Pretty soon your whole life is layered in deceit, and you can't remember the truth. Not a pretty place to live."

"It was only one lie."

"You're not helping by trying to justify it. I know last night was tricky. But you told me the truth, and I didn't get all worked up, did I?"

"You don't really think Mom would have appreciated my *shenanigans* if I'd told her the truth, do you?"

"No, probably not, but only because we've not been honest with her. If she knew about California, and knew why you were all covered in mud, she would have been okay. But she doesn't know, because we haven't told her."

"Dad, you can't. You promised—"

"I know. I'm not going to throw you under the bus. I did the same as lying by not telling her the truth and shining that flashlight in her face so she couldn't see what a mess you were. Now you've got me right smack in the middle of it, which is exactly what you said you didn't want."

"I'm sorry." I really was, but not enough to tell Mom about

California. Not yet. "Dad, why were you at Mr. McMurtry's the other day?"

"You're my daughter. It's my responsibility to be aware."

"Aware of what? He isn't bad. He's not like what everyone says."

"I know he's not bad. I stopped in to say hello and be sure he was okay with you being there."

"He loves California."

The corner of his mouth twitched. "I'm sure he does, Pumpkin. No doubt in my mind. Now go get those clothes washed, and take these towels before Mom gets up and we have some explaining to do."

After breakfast I barricaded myself in my room and spread everything from the satchel on the bathroom floor. Most of the papers I'd brought were safely sealed inside a plastic bag, but the manilla envelopes and their contents were soaked. I carefully peeled papers and cards apart and lay them in front of the old heater to dry. Two of the cards had *With Deepest Sympathy* embossed on the front, but whatever messages had been written inside would never be read again. The ink had smeared like blot tests.

Inside the bag was a handful of feed-store receipts signed in curly script by Margaret McMurtry; five report cards from a private school in town; a homemade Father's Day card with a brown pony crayoned on the front; a long, greenish frond from a tree pressed onto paper and covered with clear sandwich wrap; and a police report with Borough of Elm Lake, New York, stamped across the top. August 14, 1986. The report said a juvenile, age sixteen, had been brought in for climbing the water tower. The charge was misdemeanor trespassing. Margaret McMurtry had been claimed by her father, Mr. Jody McMurtry, and the charges were dropped.

I folded the report and leaned against the bathroom wall. It was all like what Mom kept in my treasure box at home, but so very different. Piper'd had ponies. She bought them feed at a real feed store. She loved her father, was arrested for a misdemeanor, and people had sent them cards like they had to us when Grandmother Stockton passed away. Who had died?

SEVENTEEN

Shortly before noon the hum of rain on the roof stopped. I looked outside, hoping for a rainbow or some other sign that everything would be okay when I told California about the ruined papers. Not a hint of color, not even the promise of sunshine in the still-gray sky. I shoved the satchel under my bed and left without it. When I got to the river, California was already there, sitting cross-legged under the shelter with Field's chin on her knee. He thumped his tail when I scooted in beside her—two little thumps that made me feel like part of something much bigger than anything that came before.

"He seems better."

"Yeah," she mumbled.

"You okay?" She wiggled her hand. *So-so.* "Did you come back to check on him last night?"

"Middle of the night. It was pouring rain. I'm lucky Grandfather didn't catch me. He was in the kitchen when I got back, making his special tea."

"Because of his cancer?"

"I guess." Vague circles hung below her eyes.

"You look really tired."

"I'll live."

"Did you get to Skype with Piper?"

"Why all the personal questions? Can't you just take care of his leg?"

She acted like she already knew I'd ruined the papers. I ignored the sour feeling in my gut and took out the supplies. Her mood jangled my nerves so much, I jabbed Field with the scissors by mistake. She didn't even notice.

"You should go home and sleep," I said.

"It's a headache, that's all." She fumbled around with a lump under her T-shirt. "Look who I brought."

Lacy poked her frightful head out, then jumped onto California's knee. Field opened one eye, and Lacy bobbled innocently toward his jaws. I put my hand between them.

"He could swallow her with one gulp if he wanted."

"He won't. Watch."

She was right. Field sniffed Lacy, thumped his tail, and

never flinched when the ugly chick pecked at the fur on his face.

California was so out of sorts she didn't even ask me about the satchel, and I certainly didn't bring it up. We didn't go searching for the ponies, either. Instead, we sat by the river and watched Field and Lacy make friends. After a while, we trucked slowly back through the woods. At the bottom of the hill, California stopped short in front of me.

"Uh-oh."

Mr. McMurtry was watching us. "Catherine," he bellowed.

"I'm coming," she yelled. "He thought I was sick and was going to stay in bed all day."

Mr. McMurtry met us halfway down the hill. "Catherine isn't feeling well today, Annabel. Perhaps the two of you could see each other another time." He looped an arm around her waist. California pulled away.

"It's *Annie*, Grandfather. Please. Why do you keep calling her Annabel?"

"Annie, then," he said.

When we got to the kitchen door, California motioned toward the woods with her head. "Tonight?"

Mr. McMurtry scowled. "You girls don't need to do anything tonight. Tomorrow is soon enough."

But I knew what she meant. She wanted me to take care of Field, to sneak out of my house, traipse down the road in the dark, make my way through the orchard, and potentially get lost in the woods to give Field his food and medicine.

I thought of the ruined papers and dipped my head very slightly.

Yes, I would go. Somehow I'd figure it out and would go.

The most rebellious thing I'd ever done before this summer was to fake sick so I didn't have to dance in a ballet recital. I reasoned it was a favor to Mom and Dad, so they didn't have to sit through the humiliation of watching other girls float and twirl on their toes, while I clomped around on flat feet with the jerky motions of a marionette. Faking sick was simple—a little belly holding, a few tears, the illusion of pure misery, and pulling the covers over my head. Sneaking out was an entirely different plane of deception. This required serious planning.

Outside my window the evening sun eased its way across a cloudless sky. There would be no rain tonight to stifle the sound of my escape. I picked at the hairs on the back of my neck and watched the cedar tree waving its branches back and forth.

Come, Annie, they whispered. *Come.*

Long branches brushed against the side of the house—*scritch-scratch, scritch-scratch, scritch-scratch.* That noise used to scare me when I was little. Mom always carried on about cutting down the cedar, but Dad refused. It was part of the house when he was growing up, and, except that it had been planted a little too close, it did no harm.

I scrambled across my bed and rolled the window open.

The flat peak of the gable was exactly the right width for my knees. I wouldn't have to risk making the floorboards on the stairs creak if I went out this way. Were cedar branches sturdy enough to hold me? Could I make it? Was I crazy? Did I have the courage to try?

Before we'd left for the lake, Dr. Clementi and I had talked a lot about my fear of going into eighth grade in the fall.

"What are you afraid of?"

"All those kids. The crowds."

"What about them?"

I hated when he made me come up with my own answers. Wasn't he supposed to tell me how to fix what was broken?

"They'll look at me like I'm a freak."

"Annabel, all eighth graders feel like freaks. It's required."

"They don't all have panic attacks, and they know I did. They *saw* me. What if it happens again in front of them?"

Dr. Clementi had rested his elbows on his knees. "Now we're getting somewhere. This I can understand."

A lesson loomed.

"Who is someone you admire, someone from history?"

I'd slumped in my seat, not in the mood for that.

"Okay," he'd said. "Since you love to read so much, how about a fictional character you admire?"

That made more sense. I'd sat straight up and announced, "Scout Finch, from *To Kill a Mockingbird*."

Dr. Clementi had made a temple with his fingers. "Good choice, Annabel. Little Scout Finch. What about her?"

"She faced all those people coming after her father because she knew he was doing the right thing."

"What else?"

"She got over being afraid of Boo Radley."

"Why was she afraid of Boo Radley?"

"Because he was different, and scary."

"Exactly. And what do you think helped her do these brave things?"

When I didn't answer, he'd pointed to a framed calligraphy on the wall and read out loud. "Courage is the resistance of fear, the mastery of fear, not the absence of fear."

"I don't have as much courage as Scout."

"Well, guess what? It only takes a few seconds of courage to start something that seems impossible. Then you're in."

Two or three seconds of courage. That's all it would take. Then I'd be in.

EIGHTEEN

At dinner I yawned really big, really obvious. Dad covered his mouth.

"Stop. Yawning is contagious."

"Sorry." I rubbed my eyes. "I'm really tired."

Mom cut her asparagus into one-inch slivers and dipped each feathery end into hollandaise sauce. "Maybe it's a good night for all of us to go to bed early."

I smiled inside and propped my chin on my fist for effect. *Yes! Everyone into bed early so I can sneak out.*

"Elbow," Mom said.

"May I be excused?"

"You haven't eaten anything."

Her tone left no room for argument. I jabbed my fork into the asparagus, poked it through a piece of lamb, dunked it in some gravy, put the whole thing in my mouth, and chewed. Then I ate a piece of roast potato and another bite of lamb, which almost got stuck going down.

"Is that enough? I'm going to bed."

Dad glanced at the clock. "It's only seven thirty."

"I know. I'm going to do some of my summer reading." I pushed back my chair. "The books they assigned are boring. I'll probably be asleep in half an hour."

"What books are boring?" Dad asked.

"Well, not boring. I've already read them. Jane Austen."

"Jane Austen—impressive for an eighth-grade list."

Mom sat a little taller. "Not for Annabel."

"Not for Annie, either," I said. "Good night."

"Night, Pumpkin. Happy reading."

"Good night," Mom said. "Give Mr. Darcy my best."

At eight o'clock the phone rang. At eight fifteen Mom poked her head in my doorway and said they were going to the Maxwells' for dessert.

Great. Super-duper. They were going to eat pie, which meant I'd have to wait before sneaking out. They never, ever left me alone at night without checking on me when they got back. But Field would be hungry. He needed medicine, and they were going to eat pie. The last time they went to the Maxwells' for dessert, they stayed past midnight. I worried about what would happen to Field if I had to wait that long to give him his medicine.

The numbers on my clock rolled over every sixty seconds. I watched for an entire hour, hoping to hear the sound of the Volvo putzing up the driveway. The waiting only made me more restless. If I left now while they were out, I wouldn't have to climb down the tree.

"Okay, Scout, bring on some of that courage."

Working quickly, I shoved three rolled-up towels, end to end, under my covers and laid a stuffed bear near the pillow, then stepped back to see if it would fool anyone. It wasn't good enough. I arranged *Sense and Sensibility* on the covers to look like I'd fallen asleep reading. Still not enough. I laid my Story Notebook open on the table with a pen on top, grabbed my backpack, and headed for the door.

Scritch-scratch-scritch-scratch.

With one foot inside my room, the other out in the hallway, I stopped and looked back at the windows over my bed, at the cedar tree right outside, its dark branches within easy reach.

If you're gonna be a little wild and a lot brave, you might as well go all the way.

I closed the door, rolled the window open, pushed the screen out, and crawled onto the gable, edging along on hands and knees, keeping my attention focused on the linear trunk hidden behind softly swaying boughs of green.

Scritch-scratch, scritch-scratch, scritch-scratch.

The branches thick enough to hold me were only an arm's

length away from the end of the gable. One grab, one leap, one step. Two seconds of courage, and I was in. A flash of fear rushed through me, and I swayed.

Don't look down.

This was crazy. I balanced myself and tried to swallow. After a moment of surprising calm, a surge of adrenaline pushed through me, and I was a panther, moving from the gable to the limb to the center of that tree all in one breath. The limb bent under my weight. I braced my feet on two unevenly spaced branches. The tree rocked. The backpack slipped off one shoulder. I was going to throw up.

Don't look down, don't look down, don't look down.

Then, of course, there they were. Mom and Dad and the blue Volvo, inching their way up the steep driveway and parking. Right. Below. The. Tree.

Crap.

I could hear the lurch of Dad pulling the emergency brake. One door opened. The other door opened. One door closed, then the other. They were standing right underneath me. The tree rocked, and I gripped tighter. Then Mom, with her relentless need for order, whined, "I wish you would agree to get rid of that cedar. It's a wonder Annabel gets any afternoon sun. Look how it's stuffed so close to the house."

No. Don't look at it. Go inside.

"It gives the house character," Dad said.

"It's so unsightly."

The unsightly cedar seesawed side to side. I hugged it so

tight my fingers numbed. I almost let go and dropped right in front of them. My brain refused to function properly.

Breathe in, breathe out.

The front door opened and closed. A light inside turned on.

Breathe in, breathe out.

I knew their routine. They would check the deck door, turn on the light over the stove, and in three minutes they would be upstairs—the longest three minutes of my life. The cedar fronds poked me in the face. I shifted, and prickly bark scratched my arms and cheek. Bits of it fell into my T-shirt. My feet cramped, my fingers ached, but none of that mattered because when I looked back through my window, a wedge of light from the hallway shone into my bedroom. The outline of Mom's head was just inside the door. She was looking right where the fake-me rose from my bed like a lump.

One beat. Two beats. Three beats. Four beats. Five beats.

The door closed. The wedge disappeared.

My arms shook so badly they wouldn't hold me in that tree much longer. I found the next branch with my right foot, felt around with my left, branch by branch, limb by limb, breath by breath. I got almost to the bottom and—

Snap!

Crack!

Thud!

"Ah!"

My left side hit the ground right next to the broken branch.

Everything shifted. My head spun. Something warm dripped down the side of my face—blood, from right under my hairline. My flashlight and the packet of lamb I'd stolen to feed Field had rolled out of the backpack and lay next to me in the mulch. My left hip was on fire. It took more than mere courage to pick myself up without screaming. But I did, and I picked up the backpack, and the flashlight, and the lamb, and hobbled off in the dark. Anyone who might have seen me lurching down the road in the dark could have wondered if the Hunchback of Notre Dame had come to town.

NINETEEN

By the time I got out of bed the next morning, Mom and Dad were already gone. I grabbed the satchel and a bagel and headed off for California's. She was waiting for me by the river. My hip felt like elephants had paraded across it all night. I limped the last few steps and lowered myself gingerly to the ground, hoping she'd notice and be in awe of my bravery.

"Hey," I said.

She didn't notice anything except the satchel in my lap. Her eyes widened, and she pointed a shaky finger at me. "Why do you have that?"

"What do you mean?"

Her voice was gritty. "Why. Do. You. Have. That?" Emphasis on *Have*.

"I took it home, remember?"

"No, I do not remember. You were supposed to put it back."

"What?" She was making me extremely nervous. "You told me to take it home."

"I didn't tell you to take it home. I told you to put it away. All this time Grandfather could have checked and found out we'd—" She snatched it from me. You'd have thought I'd handed her a ticking bomb the way she held it away from her body, staring, her eyes bulging. "It's wet!"

"I'm so sorry. When I got home, I forgot we were going to see *Twelfth Night* in Glens Falls. I hid it under the deck so Mom and Dad wouldn't see, then we went to the theater and out for dinner, and when I got home, I was so tired I fell right asleep. There was that thunderstorm. I had to go out in the rain in the middle of the night and get it, but it was already wet. I'm—"

Blood drained from her face. "This happened because you went to the theater with your parents? Are you kidding me? Is everything ruined?" She was seething, on the verge of full-blown hysteria.

"Not everything, some things are okay, but—"

She pulled out a manila envelope. Of course, it had to be one with a stain on the outside where ink had bled through. The envelope shook in her hands.

"I can't believe this."

"I'm so sorry. Everything was all mixed up. I forgot Mom and Dad had those tickets, and they were suspicious—"

Before I could finish, she jumped up and stomped her foot in the dirt like a spoiled kid, yellow hair springing in tiny ringlets above her forehead. "Shut up. Just shut up, Annie! I don't care why you forgot. I don't care about *Twelfth-anything*! You shouldn't have forgotten! I can't believe this!"

I barely had time to blink before she stormed off. She never came back. I waited, but an hour later walked out of the woods alone, feeling like the biggest failure on Earth.

In the light of the next morning, California's reaction seemed a bit melodramatic. I'd made a mistake, and yes, some of the papers got ruined. But it was a mistake. A miscommunication. I was trying to help her, trying to do what I thought she wanted. She made me feel like I'd ruined the papers on purpose, like no matter what, I wasn't going to get it right. A quiet day apart could do us both some good.

Mom had gone off on one of her mysterious day trips to the city, and Dad was playing tennis. I had the whole house to myself. Maybe after a minibreak we could go back to the way things were before. Maybe she'd been right that day when she'd said we should stick to the original plan. If searching for other clues led to this, it could be a sign to leave it alone.

Around lunchtime, Dad came home and changed my mind about a day of solitude. I was sitting up in bed, a peanut butter and jelly sandwich in one hand, a pen in the other, with the Story Notebook open on my lap, when he poked his head in the doorway.

"Hey, Pumpkin, it's a beautiful day outside. Mom's gone until dinner. Come sail with me. We'll have a Dad-and-Daughter Day."

How could I resist such an invite? Besides, he was right. The day was jewel-tone perfect—brilliant emerald and sapphire colors splashed from earth to sky, and the sun blazed overhead like a yellow diamond. A cool breeze swept across the lake, forcing any lingering humidity away. Dad and I rigged the Sunfish and pushed off from the dock, a small cooler of birch beer in the cockpit. Birch beer was our thing. Mom didn't like it.

"North, south, or west?" he asked.

I tilted my head back and let the sun warm my face. "South," I said, not really caring.

"South it is, m'lady." He tipped a fake hat and we sailed on.

The lift and sway of the sailboat cradled me. Pretty soon the tightness in my shoulders eased, and the fight California and I'd had didn't feel as huge. It was good to be out on the lake—good to have time alone with Dad, to not talk, to sit side by side and glide over the water, watching the sail billow in the wind, like we'd done every year since I was three. We moved along at a good clip. I touched the fluttering feathers of the blue-and-yellow tell-tale with the tip of my finger.

Until this summer, Dad and I had always gone together to pick out a half dozen wind indicators. It was tradition.

"I guess you already bought all the tell-tales?" I asked.

"Got them a couple of weeks ago. You were busy, off on some exciting adventure."

"I'm sorry."

"No biggie. That's what you're supposed to do, remember?"

Half an hour and two birch beers later, we'd sailed almost the entire way to the south end, where the border of the lake curved and lily pads grew as thick as weeds.

"We're going to turn around in a minute. Pay attention so we can switch sides," Dad said.

I'd never gotten anywhere close to that part of the lake. More than once, some kid had got their rudder caught in the lily pads and been stuck for hours. The area was off-limits to junior sailors.

"Can we go a little farther?"

Dad laughed. "And get stuck on purpose so Mom has a hissy fit when we get home late?"

"We'd be doing her a favor. She wouldn't have to find something to hiss about on her own," I teased. "Besides, I don't ever remember seeing it up close with you, and juniors aren't allowed to sail down there."

"Exploring it is, then." He winked and positioned the bow slightly to the left. "When I was a teenager, we used to camp at a spot down this way. I'll see if we can get close to show you."

About two hundred yards from land, he loosed the mainsheet and let the boat drift.

"Right around that bend, if we could navigate through the lily pads, you'd see it. Just a little meadow-like thing poking out from the woods. We'd hike around from the beach and have a campfire. Took us hours getting through the woods, but worth every blister. Some of my favorite memories from growing up took place on those nights."

"What, did you take girls down there?"

"Awww, Pumpkin, answering that would be going against the boy-code."

"Eeewwww gross, sorry I asked. Never mind, I don't need to see it."

Dad ruffled my hair and laughed. "Wish I could. Haven't been since I was a teenager."

He turned the boat, we switched sides and sailed away from Dad's childhood memory. I looked back once, but all I could see was the regular edge of the lake and the national forest that went on forever beyond.

TWENTY

California was waiting for me in the orchard.

"I'm sorry," I said as soon as I was close, eager to get the ruined-papers discussion out of the way.

She crinkled her nose. "I don't know what you're talking about. Come on. Field is gonna be hungry."

I followed her silently down the hill toward the woods, puzzled. Why was she pretending nothing had happened? At the beginning of the trail, she swung around to face me.

"I know you think I'm crazy for getting all bent the other day, Annie, but you're lucky to have your whole family together, and you don't even appreciate it."

"What? Living with my parents isn't all theater and lemon pies, you know. Most of the time I hate my mother. She isn't anything like Piper."

"But she's here. Every day you go home and they're both waiting for you, cooking for you, taking you to the theater, talking to you. I can't even talk *about* Piper without Grandfather getting all dark and storming away like I've soiled the air. He makes me feel ashamed of her. When I'm with Piper, she doesn't want to talk about him, either. Your parents, they're in your house, together, when you go to sleep at night. No one is sick. No one's been mad for all these years. And you don't even care."

She stalked off down the path without saying anything about our misunderstanding. Nothing about the papers getting wet. What she had been upset about all had to do with family.

The rest of the morning was quiet. Field came out from under the shelter and was much more active than he had been two days before. California held him steady while I checked him over.

"You'd better change the bandage today," she said. "I have to go to the city tomorrow. Piper's meeting us. Can you feed him? Saturday, too. We'll be back, but Grandfather probably won't be feeling well."

"Sure," I said, grateful I could do something to make up for ruining the papers.

I finished with Field, and we went on a search for the

ponies, taking a bag of fresh apples and scattering them strategically in places California thought they might find them and where we could easily check later to see if they'd been eaten. After a nearly silent hour we were back at the river. It felt good to do something normal again after the mess of the last week.

"I brought lunch," she said. "Are you eating at home or only when you're here? Because you're going to have to eat at home too. I can't fix everything, you know."

The corners of her mouth turned up in a sly smile. She handed me a sandwich and took a giant bite of hers.

California was back.

I was fast asleep when my cell phone beeped, stopped, then beeped again. The clock said eleven fifty. Almost midnight. It must have been a mistake. I bunched up my pillow under my head and closed my eyes. A minute later it beeped again. California's number flashed on the screen, then disappeared. I held the phone in my hand, and as soon as it vibrated, I clicked it on.

"California?"

"Can you come?" she whispered.

"Now? It's midnight."

"I know, but I leave at six in the morning. I want to see what's in the trunk before we go, in case there's something I can use to get Piper to come back. I don't want to do it alone. Will you meet me?"

I thought of the ruined papers, and of Scout Finch facing her fears to stand up for someone else. Mom and Dad were already in bed. If I was really quiet, I could sneak down the stairs instead of climbing the cedar tree again. I'd already proved I could do that.

"Okay, I'll come."

Click. She hung up without even saying good-bye.

It took me almost half an hour to get to the farm in the black night. California was already upstairs, waving the flashlight beam back and forth in front of the big window. Not that there'd be too many people standing in the middle of the road after midnight to see such a thing, but still . . .

Inside, she pointed to a pile on the floor. "You go through those," she said. "I'll do the rest."

We sat side by side, sifting, inspecting, and sorting. I organized my stuff into stacks according to type: newspaper articles, letters, photos, and memorabilia. California read one thing and tossed it aside. Read another and tossed. Eventually she looked like she was sitting in a paper replica of her front yard. I forgot all about my system when I emptied the contents of a fat manila envelope marked KMM/MKM on the floor.

On top of the pile was an obituary of someone who looked like an older version of the lady in the photograph on the tri-cornered table. The same lady California had said must have been her grandmother.

"I might have something here."

She shone her flashlight on the old clipping from the *New York Times.* The lady in the picture smiled at us with perfect teeth, and dark hair cut short in a bob. The name underneath was printed in bold letters: KATHERINE MARGARET McMURTRY.

"What's the date?"

I looked closer at the yellowed paper. "The date on top says September third, nineteen eighty-six."

California took it from me and read out loud. "'Dr. Katherine Margaret McMurtry, age fifty-one, passed away suddenly on September first during an event at the Lake Eleanor Marina in East Blue, New York. She is survived by her husband, Joseph (Jody) Woodrow McMurtry, fifty-two, and their daughter, Margaret Katherine McMurtry, sixteen. Dr. McMurtry was a leader in cutting-edge medical research during the nineteen sixties and founded the Institute for Cancer Research and Understanding in New York City before retiring from the medical field in nineteen seventy-four. She continued to serve on the board of directors until her passing. Services are pending.'"

California stopped and studied her grandmother's face. "She did cancer research. She was a doctor. That's why—"

"Why what?"

"Nothing, well, probably why— Never mind, doesn't matter. She died when Piper was sixteen. That's when she left home. I wonder if there was a connection?"

"Let's see what else we can find," I said.

There were more obituaries, each one ending the same way, "Services are pending." They'd been printed in newspapers across the country, which we thought was weird until we found the stack of missing person bulletins. Eleven altogether, published in papers from Maine to Texas, Florida to California. The first one was from September twentieth, nineteen eighty-six. The last one was dated February fourteenth, nineteen eighty-seven. Front and center on each notice was the photo of Piper with the two ponies at the horse show.

"So the question is," California said, "did she leave home before or after her mother died?"

By the time we finished going through everything in the packet, the sequence of events seemed less vague. A death certificate said heart failure. An article in the local town paper said it happened in the middle of the year-end sailing awards banquet, held at the lake on Labor Day weekend. Mrs. McMurtry had collapsed after an argument with a family member who had since disappeared. Because the person was a minor, her name was withheld for privacy.

"Nothing private about this tabloid-worthy piece of you-know-what," California grumbled. She was shaken up.

There were sympathy cards, like the ones I'd already found and got wet, and a dozen long letters. Most of the people who wrote offered to "help look for Margaret." In one, a minister had counseled Mr. McMurtry not to dwell on the things he'd said to his daughter that night, that "surely she would soon understand he was reacting to his wife's sudden death when he blamed her for it, and when she did, she would return home, God willing."

"That pretty well sums it up, I guess," California said when we were finished. "Piper and her mother had a fight, her mother had a heart attack and died, and Grandfather blamed her, so she ran away."

Instead of opening my mouth and having something stupid come out, I started putting things back the way we'd found them. Mr. McMurtry's sadness made sense now. The way he looked like it hurt to be happy, the way he was so protective of California but still kind of distant, or formal. He'd lost his family, his wife and daughter, both at the same time. He'd been alone for years, much longer than we'd even lived. That was a long time to hurt.

We were on our way out of the carriage house when California stopped and asked quietly, "Do you think he still blames Piper?"

"I don't know," I said. "It doesn't feel like it, but I don't really know."

"Yeah," she said.

"Can you ask her?"

"I don't think so, unless I can figure a way to bring it up without her knowing I know. There's still something missing here. Something important. Keep thinking on it. I'll see you Sunday."

****

Images of Piper and Mrs. McMurtry having a fight in the middle of the awards banquet, of Mrs. McMurtry collapsing, her heart giving out, dying right there in front of everyone, followed me all the way home. I was finally drifting off to sleep when a thought startled me upright.

Could that kind of thing happen in my family?

TWENTY-ONE

My whole body was a bundle of nerves before I got out of bed the next day. If Field hadn't needed food, I easily could have pulled the covers over my head and slept until noon. But he did need food, and I couldn't mess up again. I slid my feet into my slippers and was headed to the bathroom when Dad knocked.

"Pumpkin? You ready?"

Ready for what? I flung the door open and there he was, dressed in freshly ironed tennis whites, holding a racket in one hand and tossing a fluorescent-yellow ball in the other.

"Uh-oh. You forgot we have a court reserved for nine o'clock."

"I forgot."

"You keep forgetting things. It's the first time we're playing all summer. Mom made a bacon frittata. She's waiting downstairs."

My tongue stuck to the roof of my mouth. Dad tossed the ball and caught it, tossed and caught it. Sweat broke out on my forehead. His face shifted. After bouncing that ball at least a dozen times, he leaned close and whispered, "I wouldn't recommend telling Mom you forgot."

"I can't play, Dad. I'm sorry I forgot, but can you tell Mom something came up? It's kind of urgent."

He stopped tossing the ball. "Nope."

"What?"

"Get your tennis clothes on and we play, or you tell her yourself."

"Really?"

"It's your choice. I'm good either way." He bounced the racket strings lightly on top of my head. "You decide, and I'll see you downstairs."

"Dad—" But he was gone.

There was no choice. I was not telling Mom about California and Field and why they were more important than my own family. It would take less time to play the darn game and get it over with. I yanked on my stupid tennis dress, laced up my sneakers, and was on the stairs when Dad screamed.

"OOOWWWWW!!!" He writhed around on the hall floor, gripping his left ankle.

Mom careened around the corner and shoved me out of her way. "What happened?"

"It's my ankle. Mother of Mercy, this hurts."

I pressed my back against the wall while Mom helped Dad sit up.

"Annabel, bring the ice pack. Hurry!" she snapped. "And a towel—no, no, bring me a chair cushion—and a towel—two towels—hurry!"

I bolted to the kitchen and grabbed a red corduroy cushion from one of the stools, ran to the bathroom and snatched three beach towels from the closet, raced to the hall, deposited everything on the floor, and ran back to the kitchen for the ice pack.

Of course, the ice pack wasn't there. It was still down by the river, along with all the other medical supplies I'd stolen for Field. I'd never brought any of them home.

"Annabel!"

Dad mumbled something. Mom's feet pounded across the floor. "I can't be bothered with a silly name—"

She pushed me aside, shuffled around a package of peas, a gallon of ice cream, and a box of frozen cream puffs in the freezer. "Where's the ice pack? Did you take the ice pack out of here?"

I stepped back and pulled the neck of my tennis dress away from my throat, ready for her interrogation. But the oddest thing happened—

"Never mind. Get a thin towel from the drawer."

She scooped ice from the bin into a plastic bag, wrapped the towel around it, and ran back to Dad.

"Put your leg up here. No, on the cushion. I've got ice—"

"Please stop—yelling makes it hurt more."

"I'm not yelling, Richard. I'm helping you. . . ."

My stomach lurched. There must be something useful for me to do, something to make up for whatever was going on, because whatever it was, it sure felt like it was my fault. I ran hot water over the dirty dishes in the sink and picked at dried egg on the edge of a bowl. Was Dad faking so I didn't have to play tennis?

Mom screeched me out of my daze. "Annabel, the frittata is burning. I can smell it from here." Smoke billowed in a thin stream from the top of the oven door. She rushed past me, scowling. "What is wrong with you?"

The frittata emerged black and crispy. She dumped it, pan and all, into the sink, waved a towel around the kitchen, then ran back to Dad, yakking about whether to take him to the hospital or the local urgent care center.

We packed him into the backseat of the Volvo with pillows and a blanket. "Be sure the oven is turned off," Mom instructed. "I'll call you." I tried to see Dad's face before they drove away, but the pillow engulfed his head.

Minutes later I was on my way to McMurtry's farm, still wearing my white tennis dress, still sore from my fall out of the tree, still unnerved by what California and I had learned the night before. It wasn't until I got to the orchard that I realized I'd forgotten food. How stupid! I didn't want to walk the entire mile again, there and back, and no way was I going into Mr. McMurtry's house to scrounge up something. Where else could I find food?

What would Scout do?

Scout was not only a little wild and a lot brave, she was resourceful. I jogged to the back of the house. The trash bin! Dogs loved getting into people's trash. That was one of Mom's reasons for not allowing us to have one. The Rhode Island Red and the two Leghorns acted suspicious when I passed the coop, squawking like they'd already had their heads cut off. Lacy, who refused to stay inside the pen, watched from her perch on the back step. Those chickens were so weird.

The trash bin was empty—not even a scrap of leftover bread. The lid banged shut, and one of the Leghorns startled, rose up, and squawked. The other ran at the Rhode Island Red, and pretty soon all three chickens were fighting in a flurry of feathers and straw and dust. When they finally calmed down and everything settled, I saw three perfect eggs in their nests. Raw or cooked, Field would love them. Besides, it was all I had to offer.

The chickens had ugly, yellow claws at the end of scaly legs—claws that would hurt if they got the chance to dig into my flesh. California worked her way around those birds like a boss, but whenever I'd put one toe inside their territory, they'd threatened me with ruffled feathers and loud cackles. My mission called for action. I opened the gate slowly and put out a hand.

"Whoa, ugly chickens, I'm getting the eggs, same way California does."

They pushed their butts up against the wire and got real quiet. Too quiet. They were planning something. Slowly, I tiptoed inside, scooped each egg from the straw and cupped them in the hem of my tennis dress, then backed out of the pen, and ran, giggling at my success the whole way down the hill.

At the last bend in the trail, I almost tripped over Field sitting in the middle of the path, his injured leg stuck out to the side. I showed him the eggs. "Brought your breakfast. Hope you like raw eggs, 'cuz that's what you get."

His tail beat against the ground, but he didn't move.

"California's not here. You're stuck with me."

I tugged at the ruff of hair around his neck, careful to hold the eggs steady with my other hand. He made this I'm-so-sad noise and kept watching the trail. I let go of him.

"You know, I'm the one who saved your life. I'm the one who stole food and medicine and eggs and the ice pack for you, and you're still waiting for California? I'm not so sure how I feel about that."

Field whined again right as Lacy rounded the bend, flapping her wings and cackling indignantly. When she ran past us, Field turned and limped to the oak.

"So, it's Lacy you like better than me. What a sight we must be. A gimpy old dog, a crazy spotted chicken, and a city girl, all out here in the woods together with no more sense than an ant farm without a queen."

I was thinking about how impressed California would be when I told her about my adventures, how I'd knocked away one challenge after another to get Field taken care of properly. Then I saw the Rhode Island Red and two Leghorns running loose around the yard. I'd left the coop gate open. Chasing three crazy chickens into a pen they didn't want to go into, with only a broom for a weapon, was one more thing to add to my list of activities I'd never done before meeting California. It was humiliating and exciting at the same time. Another crazy summer adventure in the New-and-Improved Life of Annie Stockton.

TWENTY-TWO

For one long, delicious minute I watched the sun spread waves of apricot across the late-afternoon sky outside my window. My muscles kinked from napping in the fetal position. One at a time, I unfurled each limb and stretched like a lazy cat.

The phone rang once, twice, three times before I remembered Mom and Dad weren't home. When I'd got back, the burned-frittata disaster hadn't been touched. The smell of scorched egg still lingered in the kitchen. Mom never left the kitchen a mess, but at the time I'd been too unstrung to clean it up, and I had evidence of chicken-chasing on my clothes to wash.

Four rings. Five rings. I ran to Mom and Dad's bedroom and picked up the phone on number six. "Hello?"

Mom's voice roared through the line. "Annabel! Where have you been? I've been calling all day."

"I, um, I've been here." The cell phone lay silent on my bedside table. Dead battery. "I fell asleep. Where are you guys?"

"We'll be home after we stop at the pharmacy. They didn't have the right painkillers for Dad at the emergency room."

"Emergency room?"

There was a muffled sound when Dad took the phone from Mom. "Don't worry, Pumpkin. It's only a sprain."

Mom stuck her mouth near the phone to shout, "A sprain hurts worse than a break—"

"Vicky, stop, you're going to scare her. Watch the road," Dad said. "We'll be home in an hour, if Mom doesn't kill us on the way. I've got the shiniest pair of crutches you've ever seen."

"Dad, I don't— What—"

"Yeah, that was some fall. Completely unexpected. You'll be glad to know you're relieved of tennis duty for at least a month."

"I'm really sorry. I was going to play—"

"I know. Don't worry. Be back soon."

After we hung up, I stared at the phone. A sprain? Oh,

God, the guilt. He really was hurt. I'd let the frittata burn and run off, not even thinking he might actually be injured. What kind of person was I turning into?

By the time they pulled into the driveway, I had the kitchen spotless, the breakfast plates replaced with dinner china, and two of my own pillows lying on the coffee table for Dad to prop up his foot. I met them halfway down the steps.

"Let me help."

"No, I gotta learn how to do this." Dad braced himself on a pair of silver crutches. "I asked for wooden crutches, figured they'd go better with the lake-house decor, since we're all about decorating these days. They don't make 'em from wood anymore, only these slick, superpowered silver doohickeys."

Mom shoved a pharmacy bag into my hands. "Put this new ice pack in the freezer and get him some water. He's going to need pain pills. Hurry, Annabel."

"I don't need the ice pack. I'm good for now."

"You have a sprain. Go, Annabel."

I ignored the *Annabel* word, but paid attention to the building frenzy in her voice and ran to the kitchen.

For the first time ever, I cooked tomato soup and grilled cheese for dinner without charring the bread. Probably because Mom wasn't hovering. She fussed over Dad instead, draping towels on his lap while I carried out a tray with the soup, a golden-brown masterpiece with his favorite horserad-ish sauce on the side, and a tiny glass vase with one bright-red gerbera daisy plucked from the flowerpot on the deck.

"Thanks, Pumpkin, this is wonderful."

After a few bites the painkillers knocked him out. I carefully lifted the tray and cleaned up by myself. Mom pulled a chair next to the couch and covered herself with an afghan. By the time the dishwasher was running, they were both fast asleep.

"Mom?" I touched her arm. She opened one eye. "When you're ready to get Dad upstairs, let me know."

She nodded.

"Can I get you anything before I go up?"

She shook her head and pursed her lips. I slunk away to my room, leaving the door cracked open.

Three hours later they hadn't moved. Mom slept with her head tilted, a tiny bit of drool threatening to trickle down her chin. I dabbed it with a tissue and pulled the afghan over her shoulders. Dad's head was flung back against the sofa. There wasn't much anyone could do about his snores vibrating the walls. I turned off the lights and went back upstairs.

When I awoke on Saturday, the sun hovered high above the cedar tree outside. It was almost noon. I was late to feed Field. Very, very late.

"Oh, my gosh, oh, my gosh, oh, my gosh—" I yanked on shorts and a T-shirt, stuffed the satchel out of sight, and bolted down the stairs. Dad sat up on the couch, TV clicker in hand.

"Oh, Dad, I—"

"Well, look who's here."

"Where's— Are you okay?"

"I'm okay, Pumpkin, calm down. You sound like Mom in electric mode."

I pointed to his foot. "How's it feeling?"

He shook a prescription bottle. "The famous put-me-to-sleep painkillers are working their magic."

"Good. I'm really sorry about what happened, Dad."

I meant it. If I hadn't forgotten the tennis game, if he hadn't gone off down the stairs so fast—probably to distract Mom in case I decided not to play—none of this would have happened.

"You didn't do anything. You off on some wild adventure today?"

"Yeah, I'm late, but I can't leave you alone. Where's Mom?"

"She's at the library getting me books. Go. Vamoose. Skedaddle! Hurry, before she gets home and puts you to work coddling me."

"I—"

"Go on. I've had all the coddling I can take for twenty-four hours. Have fun."

He flipped his hand, dismissing me. I leaned over and kissed the top of his head.

"Love you, Dad."

"Ditto."

I wrapped two hefty chunks of leftover turkey breast

in foil and shifted things around inside the fridge so Mom wouldn't notice right away. Out the door and down the steps, I moved as fast as I could with my aching hip.

Poor Field, having to rely on someone who was always late, or forgot food.

Poor California, having to rely on someone who was always late, or forgetting things outside in the rain.

Poor Mr. McMurtry, alone and sad all those years.

Poor Piper, with all the pain that must have kept her away.

All of them, knowing it or not, were counting on me. I couldn't fail them again.

Breathe, Annie, breathe.

TWENTY-THREE

E ven with me keeping to the shade on the side of the road, the humidity made my heart pound. There was no stopping, though—not yet. I cut through the orchard and veered across the field toward the trailhead, putting me in plain view of the house. California had said Mr. McMurtry wouldn't be feeling well, so I figured he'd stay inside and I didn't need to worry about him seeing me.

Two-thirds of the way across the field, I stopped where a cool breeze swept over the hill. The trailhead was still a good hundred yards away, but I had to let my heart slow down and try to stop the pounding in my head. Pressing two fingers against each temple, I inhaled slowly through my nose and exhaled even slower out my mouth. I wouldn't make it to the river if the throbbing blinded me.

"Git!"

My hands jerked out, and I dropped flat to the ground.

"Git!"

Mr. McMurtry! Where was he? I slithered through the grass, trying to get a better view. *Dear God, please let Matilda not be out for a nap. Please don't let chiggers creep into my underwear. And most of all, please don't let Mr. McMurtry find me.*

He was still out of my sight, but about twenty strides away, halfway between the woods and the house, Field raised up slowly out of the grass, watching the top of the hill.

"Field," I half whispered. "Over here!" He didn't flinch.

A glint of something shiny made me turn. Mr. McMurtry strode purposefully over the crest and down the slope, pointing a long, bronze rifle at Field's head.

"Go on, dog. Get out of here."

Field's lips curled, exposing sharp, yellowed teeth. The ruff around his neck stood on end. Mr. McMurtry shook the rifle, and it made a menacing click. *No!* The word stuck in my head. My body locked. Field lowered his shoulders and stretched forward until he was only a shadow again. Mr. McMurtry stopped, raised the rifle, and laid his cheek against the metal, staring down the barrel at his target.

"Git!"

He was close enough for me to see his thumb reach for a lever on top of the rifle, then shift and aim down. Field shuffled back one step. No way could he run fast enough to escape a bullet. That bad leg would drag him to his death.

"No!" I grunted.

"Git, dog!"

Crack!

A bullet spewed grass and dirt up in the air. Field yelped and backed another few inches. Mr. McMurtry had missed. He wouldn't miss a second time. My hand shot out, flinging the foil packet of turkey through the air to distract him while I jumped up and bolted toward Field.

"No. Don't!" Field raised his head. "Get down!"

I ran straight for him, flailing my arms and screaming. A few strides away I leaped through the air, my body stretched wide, and landed hard on the ground next to him. "I'm sorry I was late, I'm sorry—" I covered Field with my body. My bruised hip stung and I rolled off it, crying, hysterical, not caring if Matilda or chiggers or even a bullet got me.

Mr. McMurtry's boots thundered down the hill, *boom-boom, boom-boom, boom-boom.* He hoisted the rifle in the air, clenched his other hand into a fist, and waved it around with a crazy expression on his face.

"Get away from that wild dog!"

"He isn't wild—he belongs to us, me and California. He's ours. His leg is torn up—he won't hurt anyone."

I seized Field's head and shoved it under my arm. Mr.

McMurtry slammed to a halt, the rifle hanging limp by his side, his mouth opened into a perfect O. His eyes shifted between the dog and me. He breathed so loud I could hear air rattling in his lungs. Tears streamed down the side of my nose.

"He's ours," I cried. "Please, don't hurt him. I was late; he was looking for food. California said . . ."

Hiccup!

"Catherine said what?" Gone was the soothing, chamomile-tea tone. His voice had turned as cold as a stone on a frozen hill.

Hiccup!

She said you'd be sick today, and she had to stay inside to help you; she said we couldn't look for the ponies. I had to come feed Field, and I was late because my dad sprained his ankle all because of me. Field was only looking for food, or for California, or maybe even me; but he wasn't going to hurt anyone . . . I promise—

"What did she say?" he demanded.

"She said you would be sick today from your treatment, and she would have to stay home, so I had to take care of him. . . ."

Mr. McMurtry's shoulders sank. He waved his hand for me to stop rambling, and the corners of his eyes dropped.

"She said I—" He squeezed two fingers along the bridge of his nose, and his whole body sagged. When he let go, he stood in front of Field and me, holding that rifle at his side, his silence screaming of something so sad, I knew I'd never forget that moment as long as I lived.

"I thought he was coming to eat the chickens." His voice had softened. "One of them is missing, the one you girls call Lacy. She won't stay in that coop. She's every bit as stubborn as Catherine. I figured the dog got her and was coming back for more."

"Lacy's gone?"

"It's going to break Catherine's heart. She carries that damn-fool bird around with her everywhere." He wiped his face in the crook of his elbow, then stretched out a hand to me. "I wasn't going to shoot the dog. I only wanted to scare him off. If he belongs to you girls, we should get him some food."

His hand was callused but warm, and he held mine for a half second longer than he needed to. I didn't mind. He turned wordlessly toward the house, motioning for Field and me to follow. At the kitchen door, he pointed to the stoop.

"The dog stays here. He can't come in."

Field flopped onto his belly, panting but comfortable, like he was used to being at someone's back door. I tried to look past Mr. McMurtry to see if California was in the kitchen, but her chair was empty. Squishing my body into the only slice of shade, I scratched the top of Field's muzzle. Mr. McMurtry came out a few minutes later and placed two ceramic bowls in front of Field, disappeared inside, and came back again with a glass of ice water for me.

"He's got a black tongue," he said. "Means he's got Chow in him."

"Is that good?"

"Doesn't mean good or bad, just a fact."

"Did you have a Chow?"

"Part. But that was a long time ago." His eyes sank at the corners.

We watched Field eat, and when he was done, Mr. McMurtry picked up the bowls and nodded at the back leg.

"How'd he get that injury?"

"Some kind of animal trap."

"Hmm. Well, Catherine isn't feeling well today. She's still sleeping." He opened the screen door. "The fumes from the train, you know, they make her sick. She probably told you that. Perhaps you could return the dog to wherever you girls keep him, and I'll try to figure out how to tell her about that chicken."

I pushed myself off the ground and grabbed Field by the ruff around his neck. "I'll take him now."

We'd only gone a few steps when Mr. McMurtry called out, "Well, what do you know?" He pointed down the hill at Lacy, who was running side to side through the grass, flapping her wings and cackling like we'd forgotten to invite her to a party.

TWENTY-FOUR

On Sunday morning California left a red shirt dangling from the lowest branch of the third apple tree in the third row from the paddock, our secret sign that she had already gone to the river. Every time I saw it, it made me smile. Coming around the last bend in the trail, I almost collided with her standing in the middle of the path, looping a string around the waist of her shorts.

"Holy Minnesota, all this running through the woods is making me skinnneeeee."

I reached for my own shorts. All I could stuff inside the gap now was the tip of my pinky. I was making progress.

"How are you feeling?" I asked.

"Great. Why?" she asked, her face all shiny and sparkly.

"Your grandfather said you weren't feeling well yesterday."

Shiny-sparkly face disappeared, replaced by dark-and-doom. "You saw him? I told you not to come to the house. Why did you come to the house?"

"I didn't. Well, not on purpose. Didn't he tell you? He almost shot Field."

"What?"

"On the hill. He thought Field was coming to eat the chickens. Lacy was missing and I was late and . . ."

I told California everything.

"Field was growling, and your grandfather pointed a rifle at his head—he shot at him, but he missed."

Her face was like stone. "Go on—"

"I ran to Field with that rifle pointed right at me, and I swear I could practically feel a bullet burn a hole through me. But he didn't shoot—he ran down the hill shouting all crazy-like for me to get away."

"Son-of-a-biscuit-eater, he was going to kill him!"

"He said he was only trying to scare him. Lacy was missing, and he thought Field had eaten her. I kept thinking about everything, and how if he knew the truth about—"

"You didn't tell him, did you?"

"Of course not. But I had to tell him Field was ours."

"What did he say?"

"He got all moody, the way he gets, and you kind of know he's somewhere else in his head. He never said anything about him being ours, just that his tongue was black and that means he's part Chow, and he needed food. That was all."

California knelt and wrapped her arms around Field's neck. "So, he knows about Field. And it's okay. That's good, Annie. I'm glad." The shiny-sparkly smile was back. "And I'm glad you didn't get hit by that bullet."

"Your grandfather said you were sick. What was wrong?"

"Puh. Egg salad."

"Egg salad?"

"Yeah, the ladies at the hospital always give me lunch. They feel sorry for me, having to traipse all over the city with Grandfather every week. They gave me egg salad. I have a rule: never eat egg salad unless I make it myself. I started puking before we even got home."

"From the train fumes?"

"Huh?"

"Your grandfather said the train fumes make you sick. Was that it? Or the egg salad?"

She swiped at the air with her hand and scowled. "Does it matter? I was sick."

I let it go. But something dark settled over me. Something I knew I'd have to think about later.

California handed me a sandwich and unwrapped hers— plain jam, made from the last of the raspberries. She took one bite, then pulled off a piece for Field.

"How was Piper?"

"Fine. Still wouldn't come here."

"I'm sorry."

"Whatever."

"So we still have the attic and your grandfather's room to go through, right?"

"You know, sometimes this all feels pointless. Maybe we should quit."

"We can't let it go now."

California sprang from the ground. "Don't you see? There's nothing that's going to help me get her home. It's a waste of time. Obviously something else happened after she left this magical-fairyland existence, something really bad that's kept her away. Grandfather tried to find her, he tried to bring her home, and she didn't come. I was thinking when we were in New York, he's never once asked her to come back. I'm the only one who cares, and I'm the only one who doesn't know why. What does he know that makes him not ask her?"

She stood in front of me with her fists pressed into her hips, her nostrils flaring and eyes wet.

"Okay, calm down. Let's think on this a little before deciding to quit. We should keep looking for the ponies until we figure something else out."

She turned away, her head down and one hand on Field as he walked beside her. She'd work off a little steam, and things would right themselves again, like they always did. I followed her deep into a cramped, dark part of the woods we hadn't explored before when my foot got stuck in a twisted vine.

"Wait up. I'm all tangled in something."

"Hurry," she mumbled. "My head is killing me."

I bent down to unravel the woody vine, and right there, right in front of me, was a pile of something that looked suspiciously like horse manure.

"Hey, what's this?"

She glanced over her shoulder. "Aren't you done yet?"

"Look!"

She followed the direction of my finger. It took a few seconds before she saw it, before all that energy she'd been using to be upset shot her forward like a racehorse bolting out of a starting gate.

"Ohmygodohmygodohmygod, they were here!" She ran to the pile, her face lit up, and big, fat tears rolled down her cheeks. "Peaches and Cream—they're real, Annie. They're still here. We're going to find them. We really are!"

California danced around on her tiptoes, pointing at the ground, laughing, and crying, and laughing even more from someplace way deep inside her. I'd seen California happy—most of the time she was happy. But this—this kind of happiness I'd never seen from anyone, anywhere, anytime. Never.

She pressed her hands, one on top of the other, against her heart. "Now she'll come home for sure."

Something whacked the back of my brain, hard.

Guilt.

Shame.

Until that second, when every bit of hope she'd been holding inside bubbled out of her and spilled like sunshine on the dark earth, I'd never really believed we would find those ponies. I never thought for sure they were still alive. And I'd never understood how desperately California believed that by finding them, her mother would come home. I never really knew how much she hurt.

My friendship with California was all about me—the adventures, the farm, the freedom it gave me from Mom— the kind of summer I'd only dreamed about. I'd gone along with all her crazy ideas because it meant I got to climb trees and swim in a river, heal a sick dog and hold a baby chick, and feel what it was like to grow up on a real farm, the way I'd always wanted. She took me away from spreadsheets, and from choking. She was healing me. It was all about me. It had never been for her.

I had never really believed.

I hadn't been a real friend.

She pushed the brown lumps around with a stick. "This is no more than a week old, Annie. The ponies could be right around the corner, or down that hill."

She took off, snapping twigs under her feet and swiping at branches. I followed close behind, not because I thought the ponies really would be right around the next bend, but because of what that tiny bit of hope did for her. And because I knew for sure there was something she wasn't telling me. Something that made bringing Piper home so much more important for her than I could imagine.

TWENTY-FIVE

I'd barely gotten inside the house when the Radcliffes' car pulled in the driveway. Mrs. Radcliffe burst through the door behind me.

"Oh, hello, Annabel. Here now, be a love, take this to your dad, would you?"

She thrust a giant basket of fruit into my arms, then disappeared into the kitchen with two bottles of clear alcohol and her *Bartender's Guide* book. A colorful *Get Well* mylar balloon bopped me in the face.

Tommy pushed the balloon aside and smiled. "Hey." No sign of Sam-from-Savannah.

"Hey," I said. We stood awkwardly in the entryway like a couple of idiots until the Gordons and the Maxwells came through the doorway.

"Hello, Annabel! Hello, Tommy!" Mrs. Gordon said in her cheery British accent. Mr. Gordon liked to tell how he imported a good English woman to marry him so he could listen to her talk for the rest of his life. As much practice as he got, I wasn't sure if he still thought it was a wise choice. "It's so good to see you, darlings, so good. Oh, my goodness, there's your mum slaving away in the kitchen, I'll go help her. Hello, Vicky . . ."

Mr. Maxwell handed Tommy a platter of sandwiches, and Mrs. Maxwell came up behind him with a vase of red tulips in her arms.

"Hello, hello, how the heck are you?"

No one waited for me to answer before heading to the kitchen. Tommy followed them, and I took the basket to Dad, who was still propped up on the couch.

"Hey, Pumpkin! We're having company. Did we tell you that?"

"No."

"Oh, well, a little get-together. Mom said it's for me, but you and I know it's really for her, right? I think Tommy's coming."

"He's here." I sat down next to him. "Do I have to stay?"

"I'd like for you to," he said. "I don't see enough of you these days. Everything going okay?"

I nodded again and rested my head on his shoulder.

"Good to know. California okay?"

I shrugged because, really, I wasn't sure. Dad squeezed my hand.

"Hey, go help Mom, okay? She's got that whole crowd in there with her. Give her a hand."

"Do I have to? She loves that attention. She doesn't need me."

"It would make her happy, Pumpkin. Would you do it, for me?"

"Okay." I sighed. "But only because you're broken."

Right as I got up, all the guests filtered into the living room, making their way straight for Dad. I made a speedy exit. Mom was alone in the kitchen putting glasses on a tray.

"Annie, there you are. We have company," she said. As if I couldn't tell. "Take these to the bar for Mr. Radcliffe. Oh, and Tommy's here." She reached for my face, started to say something, but stopped herself and frowned instead.

"No one told me you were having a party. You could have said something."

"I didn't know we were supposed to ask your permission," she said. "You may not have noticed, but the world doesn't revolve around you *all* the time."

The truth behind her words stung. I picked up the tray and went into the living room in time to hear Dad telling everyone about his fall, and something that included my name that made everyone laugh.

"Hey, Pumpkin, I was just saying how lucky you are that you don't have to play tennis with me now." He winked and motioned to his foot. Every one of them, including Tommy, turned to stare at me.

"I heard you."

They all converged on me at once, hovering a breath away, saying things like "Oh, Annabel, it's good to see you. You look terrific," and "The beach isn't the same without you there every day," and "Where have you been all summer?"

They couldn't leave it there. Mrs. Radcliffe got all up in my face, smiling really wide, a dot of red lipstick smeared on her front tooth.

"Annabel, tell us about Jody McMurtry's granddaughter. What's she like?"

Of course, Mrs. Radcliffe said it right as Mom stepped into the room holding a little china dish of sliced lemons. Her eyes practically popped out of her face, and she took a sharp breath like I'd stabbed her in the heart.

"Who?"

She didn't say it like a normal person would say *who*, but like someone on the verge of hysteria. Mom's disapproval of the McMurtrys was no secret. This was not the way I wanted her to find out about California.

But Mrs. Radcliffe couldn't leave it alone. "Jody McMurtry's granddaughter's been here all summer. You must have known, Vicky. Annabel's there all the time!"

Mom leaned against the wall, her face crimson. She stared

at Dad, who could only shrug his shoulders in response to her silent question. *Did you know?* Everyone stared, but no one spoke. No one came to my rescue. The tray shook in my hands. The glasses clinked against each other. My knees felt weak. My throat tightened, but I couldn't move out of the center of that crowd.

"I feel sick," I said.

Mr. Radcliffe grabbed the tray. Mrs. Radcliffe helped me sit down, and Mrs. Gordon brought a cold washcloth. Someone handed me a glass of water. All the while I thought of Piper having a fight with her mother, and her mother dying in front of her, in front of Mr. McMurtry, maybe even dying right in front of these same people standing in our living room.

I didn't want Mom to die. I wanted room to breathe. I wanted to make my own decisions, pick my own passions, study when I chose, and not clean my room if I didn't feel like it. I wanted to decide by myself what I would be when I grew up. I wanted to think for myself, pick my own clothes, pick my own friends. But I never wanted to do anything that would make her die.

"I'm okay, Mom. Really. I think I forgot to eat or something."

She didn't move. She stayed propped against the wall, her mouth slightly open, eyeing me like I was an unwelcome stranger.

"Drop in blood sugar will do that, hon," Mrs. Radcliffe

cooed, the sleeve of her electric-blue muumuu flapping in my face. "Get her an orange or some peanut butter, Vicky. She'll be fine." She fanned me with a magazine. Mom didn't move.

"Hey, Pumpkin," Dad said. "You okay?" He knew I wasn't. With Mom hearing this way about a secret we'd had all summer and her finding out because apparently everyone else already knew, no, I was not okay. I pulled my T-shirt away from my throat.

"I need to lie down," I mumbled. "I'm going upstairs."

Mom turned away and disappeared into the kitchen.

Mrs. Radcliffe said to Dad, "Annabel's okay, Richard. Her skin is already all pink again, see?"

A fire under my feet couldn't have made me run any faster up those stairs and into my room. I locked the door behind me, but I knew the second the last guest left, it was all over. Mom would never let me be associated with a member of Mr. McMurtry's family, especially one with a renegade mother and sperm donor father. And she would never forgive Dad or me for keeping it a secret.

But she never came. I waited, watching the evening light change the same way it always did as if nothing was wrong with the world. Shadows fell across the wall and darkened the collection of rustic, wood-framed wildflowers Dad and I had pressed when I was seven. The light slowly changed from yellow to indigo, finally settling at black. I sat alone in the dark listening for sounds that would tell me the guests had gone and Mom would be coming to do battle. She never did.

The next morning I crept downstairs and peeked into the living room. Dad was asleep sitting up on the couch, his chin dropped to his chest. The noise coming from him this time was more of a quick snort-snort-purrrr kind of thing. Every time he got to the purrrr part, he startled. One of his arms was draped protectively over Mom, who lay curled on her side, her face pressed against the back of the couch. Her clothes were rumpled, and her Ferragamo sandals had been flung carelessly under the coffee table.

I touched Dad's arm. He opened one eye and put a finger to his lips, pointing at Mom. I motioned to the door, and he waved me away.

"Are you sure?" I whispered. "Do you need me to bring you anything before I go?"

"Nope, I'm okay." He settled against the sofa again and smoothed Mom's hair with his hand.

"Dad?"

"Hmmm?"

"How well did you know California's mother?"

"She was younger than me, but the family was active at the lake when they weren't off at horse shows. She had show ponies. She moved away right after her mother died."

"Do you know why she never came home?"

He stroked Mom's forehead with the back of his hand. "No, I don't. We never really heard where she'd gone, and her father shut himself away. No one that I know of ever knew anything about her. Until now. Where do they live?"

"Oregon. On a tree farm."

"Wow, that's a long way away."

"How did Mrs. Radcliffe know about me being friends with California?"

"She told Mom she'd seen you there a few times when she drove to town."

"How'd Mom take that?"

Mom groaned and turned on her back. Dad whispered, "It's not as bad as you think. Go on about your day. Just be home early. We'll talk tonight."

He didn't have to tell me twice.

TWENTY-SIX

I worried the whole way to the farm. What if Mom woke up all crazy and decided to drive to Mr. McMurtry's to make a big scene and drag me home? Dad wouldn't be able to stop her since he was broken. The last thing I wanted was to add more drama to California's and Mr. McMurtry's lives. They'd had enough. So had I.

I found them both behind the house. Mr. McMurtry puttered around in those big, black boots that used to scare me. Now, after spending so many weeks of the summer around him, I loved those boots. They always had bits of earth from the herb garden or slivers of corn silk stuck to the heels. Mom would scoff at those boots if she saw them, like she scoffed at the unsightly cedar tree.

Field lay sprawled in front of the doghouse Mr. McMurtry had built, lapping water from a bowl. The only thing left from his injury was a limp Mr. McMurtry said would probably be permanent. California came out of the chicken coop with a basket over one arm. Her hair was braided into two thick chunks, her cheeks pink again, and when she saw me trotting down the driveway, she held up the basket to show me two white and two pale-brown eggs on the bottom.

"Grandfather, can Annie have breakfast with us?"

Mr. McMurtry stopped and bowed his head. "Good morning, Annabel. Of course, Catherine. If Annabel can stomach my pancakes, she is more than welcome."

He took the basket and disappeared inside the kitchen. Their cheerfulness put me at ease. Surely, Mom couldn't complain about a friendship with people this nice.

"Catherine, Annabel, ugh." California smacked her forehead. "I guess we have to pick and choose our battles, right? He isn't ever going to call us by our real names. We should make something up for him, something funny, that only we'll understand."

I clicked my heels and saluted. "How about the Captain?"

California tilted her face toward the sun and laughed. Lacy flew from the coop and perched on top of a post, ruffling her new feathers. Field wandered over and sniffed my hand, asking for treats. The smell of bacon and coffee drifted from the kitchen. How could anything bad have ever happened on that farm?

"He's going to buy fencing supplies this morning," she whispered before we went in. "As soon as he leaves, we'll check out the attic and his room. I feel positive we're going to find something important today. I know it, Annie. Don't you?"

Inside, Mr. McMurtry ladled batter onto a griddle with one hand and lifted thick slices of bacon from a pan with the other. Butter sizzled in a cast-iron skillet on the back burner. A jar of periwinkle wildflowers rested on the windowsill, and every few minutes he stuck his nose in them. Something was different, something I couldn't see, only feel. The entire room vibrated with happy. I cleared a chair and sat down.

"Grandfather, can you make Annie one with the funny face?"

"Do we have berries?" He flipped a pancake and drizzled bacon grease around the edge.

She handed him a clear bowl piled high with blueberries. "Here you go, Captain." She patted his shoulder lightly, then went to the fridge and poured us each a glass of orange juice, picked a handful of forks and knives out of a basket on the counter, and laid them on the table along with three plates.

"Hey, look, the silverware matches."

"Lucky day," Mr. McMurtry said.

California sat down and smiled. "Oh, you don't even know how lucky."

It was amazing what the proof of the ponies we'd found had done for her. Everything shone. She was one hundred percent happy-go-lucky California.

"The corn is ready." She handed me a bowl of steaming yellow cobs. "We eat it at every meal. Have to or it'll waste."

She motioned to a basket on the floor overflowing with fat, unshucked ears. "Grandfather, what did you do with all the corn before I was here to eat it?"

Mr. McMurtry brought a large platter of pancakes to the table. The top one had blueberry eyes, a mouth, a nose, and small pancake ears. He slid five fried eggs around the edge of the same platter and piled a dozen slices of bacon on top of them. But he never answered her question.

"Help yourself, ladies."

California gave me the happy-face pancake, then loaded her plate with four of her own, two eggs doused with hot sauce, and four pieces of bacon. She gobbled up everything, along with a large bowl of blueberries in cream, two cups of coffee—I'd never seen a kid drink coffee before—and two ears of corn slathered with butter and seasoned salt.

We were almost done when Mr. McMurtry handed her a pill bottle and motioned for her to open it.

"Ugh, vitamins." She downed three large, oval pills with the last of her juice. "Don't you think, with everything I just ate, that I got enough good-for-me food to last a week?"

Mr. McMurtry held his knife and fork over a piece of bacon and said, "No, Catherine, I do not."

California jabbed the air with her fork. "Argh! You're so evil."

"Perhaps."

"Do you have to take vitamins, Annie?"

"Mom used to make me take cod liver oil every day. She finally stopped when I threw it up all the time."

Mr. McMurtry kept cutting, chewing, and wiping his mouth with a napkin; but I could tell, behind all that hair and those proper manners, he was laughing at us.

"That's worse than gross, right?" California said. "Grandfather, are we excused?" Without waiting for an answer, she pushed back her chair and took both our plates to the sink.

"Remember your chores."

"Aye, aye, Captain." California saluted.

"Annabel, it was lovely to have such polite company this morning. You are welcome anytime. Give my regards to your father."

"I will. Thank you for the nice breakfast."

He stood up when I did, dipped his head, and sat back down.

TWENTY-SEVEN

California paused at the gate leading to the paddock and ran her hand through a mass of white, star-shaped blossoms that fell across the top of the wood slats.

"Piper planted this jasmine. She used to sit here and write poems. That's the only thing Grandfather ever told me about her, and the only reason he told me that is because he saw me out here with the pruning shears one day, ready to cut. He freaked out."

She jerked the half-rotted post upright and stuck her nose deep into the flowers.

"I didn't even know she wrote poetry." She ducked her

chin and pushed through the gate to the paddock. "There's so much she never told me."

Mr. McMurtry's car pulled onto the road. He honked twice, driving off toward town. California brightened instantly.

"Game time!"

We ran through the kitchen, down a hallway, past a creepy living room with furniture covered by plastic sheets, and drapes closed so tight not a sliver of sunlight could break through. California stopped halfway down the hall.

"Attic first. Climb on my back, then pull that string hanging from the ceiling," she said, dropping to hands and knees.

I took off my shoes and climbed up, bracing myself with my hands on the wall on each side. "Easier than climbing a tree that first time," I said.

Grabbing the string tight, I eased the door downward.

"Pull on the bottom of that ladder—that's how I saw Grandfather do it—and once it starts unfolding, jump because it'll fall down pretty fast."

I pulled until I felt it give. "Okay, got it."

We jumped out of the way right before the ladder planted a leg in the middle of her back. I followed her up into the dark, cramped space. The ceiling was barely high enough for us to stand, too dark to see anything. California took a miniature flashlight from her pocket.

"Always be prepared," she said, shining the tiny beam around the empty room until it landed on a large wooden crate pushed against the far wall.

"Jackpot!" We crept to the other end of the attic. "This is it. I can feel it. Here, hold this for me. Shine it right there," she said, pointing.

"I feel like Nancy Drew."

"Nancy Drew's got nothing on us."

It took a lot of heaving to open the crate, but finally the top rested against the wall. I shone the light inside.

"What the—" California lifted out a bottle and studied the label. "Wine. From France." She put that bottle back and pulled out a second one. "Exactly the same."

Bottle after bottle was identical. Same year, same vineyard.

"I can't believe this," she said. "Bottles of wine and nothing about his own daughter." She snatched the flashlight from me and moved the beam around the room again. "Let's get out of here. I feel sick."

We climbed out of the attic, folded the ladder, and pushed the door closed. California looked beaten. Dark circles I hadn't noticed before hung underneath her eyes.

"Nothing up there. Useless waste of our time," she grumbled.

"There's got to be something in his room."

"Why? Because no one erases everything about their own kid's life except a few ribbons and photos stashed away inside a trunk in some super secret closet?"

Mr. McMurtry's bedroom could have been a hotel room for all the stuff that *wasn't* there. No pictures, no papers, no television, just a double bed made up with hospital corners—the same precise way Mom had taught me—a dresser with a small wood-framed mirror over it, one rung-backed wicker chair pushed against a wall between two curtainless windows, and a small, oval braided rug on the floor. California went right to the dresser and started riffling through the drawers.

"You search in there," she said, waving toward the closet. "Check the floor and walls for loose boards or openings."

Mr. McMurtry's clothes hung neatly on hangers. Two pairs of old shoes were tucked underneath, alongside a small, sturdy step stool. A cane hung from a nail on the wall. Nothing else. No boxes, no extra coat hangers, no cedar trunk for sweaters, nothing like what Mom and Dad had in their closet. When I came out, California's feet projected from under the bed.

"What are you doing?"

"Checking to see if there's a secret compartment under the mattress," she said. "Nope, nada." She scooted out. "Any luck in there?"

I shook my head. "It's almost empty."

She sat up and rested her back against the bed, her shoulders slumped. "Dagnabbit! I felt sure we'd find something in here. Nothing in there at all?"

"Just regular clothes-type stuff, and a step stool. That's it."

"There's a step stool in there?"

"Yeah, a wooden one."

"Annie, if there's a step stool, there's going to be some-thing up high." She pushed me out of her way, set the stool in front of the hanging clothes, and climbed up, shining the flashlight on a shelf.

"Hand me that cane! There's something up here."

Pushed way to the back was a small, metal box. She set it on Mr. McMurtry's bed, brushed dust from the top with her hand, and tried to open it.

"Locked up tight, of course," she grumbled.

I turned the box over. Taped to the bottom was a small, silver key. "That's where I keep the key to my diary. Taped underneath."

It fit perfectly.

"Annie-girl, you're brilliant. Did I ever tell you that?"

California opened the lid, and her skin instantly drained, as if someone had unplugged her. Parcels of envelopes, tied together by faded pink ribbons, were stacked neatly inside. With shaky hands, she picked up a packet and pulled the ribbon loose.

"Letters. That's Piper's handwriting. The postmarks— Pennsylvania, Ohio, Nebraska, Wyoming, and look at the dates. She wrote these on her way to Oregon. This whole bunch." Turning one over, she peeked inside, her eyes widen-ing. "He opened them—he's read these."

She grabbed another batch and checked the front of five envelopes. "These are all from a post office box in Eugene.

That's about an hour from where we live in Oregon."

There were two more bundles, all tied with the same kind of pink ribbon.

"These last couple of letters are from right before I was born. Nothing recent, though. Nothing about—"

The screen door in the kitchen slammed. Mr. McMurtry!

California shoved the letters into the box, threw it back on top of the shelf, and pushed me out of his room, across the hall to hers, all in about two seconds.

"Why is he home so soon?" I whispered.

"No idea, just go out through the window," she said. "I don't want him to know we were inside and ask what we were up to."

"Am I not allowed to be—"

"Just go!"

She held the curtains back for me to escape. Of course, I knocked the desk lamp over trying to get out so fast. I don't know if Mr. McMurtry heard it fall—I was halfway home before he'd have made it to California's bedroom to investigate.

TWENTY-EIGHT

Someone tapped on my door. Before I could get up, Dad pushed it open with one of his crutches, the other wedged under his armpit.

"Made it up the stairs in record time. Come on down, Pumpkin. Let's have dinner and talk this out so we can move on, okay?"

"Dad, can I skip—"

"No. That's not fair to anyone." He turned away.

The dining-room table was set with the good china and linens. Mom sat stiffly at one end and made a big production of unfolding and laying her napkin in her lap so she didn't have to look at me. I took my seat, and Dad offered me a glass bowl of fresh-cut fruit salad.

"Fruit?"

At the same time, Mom held out a crimped porcelain dish.

"Quiche?"

My hand hovered awkwardly in the air between them. It felt like a tug of war. Dad quickly set the fruit bowl on the table, and I grabbed the quiche dish. First tricky moment out of the way.

"Annabel. I mean, Annie—" Mom twisted her wedding ring. "I apologize for not helping you last night when you weren't feeling well. I was in a bit of a shock myself."

She was apologizing to me? Who was this mom? Just as quickly, she ruined a perfectly marvelous moment.

"It's always you and Dad together with your secrets," she said. "I feel like an outsider in my own family. I've tried so hard this summer to be the mom you wanted. You can't imagine how difficult this has been. Then I find out about your friendship with the McMurtrys' granddaughter, and to make it worse, you confided in Dad and left me out again. Apparently everyone at the lake knew except me."

I pulled the neck of my T-shirt. Her nostrils flared at the edges, but she leaned back in her chair, placed her hands neatly in her lap, and pressed her lips together.

"Mom, you always talk bad about Mr. McMurtry. California's the best friend I've ever had, and I didn't want you to say mean stuff about her. Mr. McMurtry loves her. He does, and he's good to her." My voice cracked. "There's something wrong. I have to help her get her mother to come back. She doesn't know—"

I'd worked myself up into such a frenzy that my face was wet. I choked on the rest of my words. Mom handed me a box of tissues.

"Her mother isn't what you think," I sobbed. "She helps run a really big tree farm, and she's smart. She homeschooled California and taught her about wood and trees and nature and the stars and math—California's better at math than I am, and she's never even been inside a school—"

"I'm sure she is very bright," Mom said. "Her mother was very intelligent. Lively and undisciplined, but smart."

It took a moment for me to digest what she had said. "You knew her?"

Mom tipped her head. "I only met her twice, but I heard a lot about her from Grandmother Stockton. She didn't approve of the way Margaret was being raised. Too much freedom, she always said." She gave Dad an I-told-you-so look. "Too much freedom can ruin a child, you know."

She swished in her seat, like what she had announced was fact, and no one should argue with her because she knew everything. She was talking about me, and I couldn't stay silent. Not anymore.

"Well, no freedom will choke your kid. Did you know that, Mom? Did you know I almost choked to death every time I ate because you had me so squished into a . . . a . . . mold or something, I couldn't breathe or swallow any food? That's why I couldn't eat. You do realize that, don't you?" My voice had gone up two octaves. "You did it. You made me sick!"

Mom jolted upright like I'd slapped her, then planted her face in her hands. Dad's fist slammed the table.

"Annabel! Stop! That is completely unfair!" His face was redder than the watermelon in the fruit salad. "Apologize to your mother right now!"

"Apologize for what?"

He thrust his finger near my face. "For saying something so blatantly hurtful. That's uncalled for. Your mother has done everything she could all summer to try to make you happy. Now get ahold of yourself and apologize before we all have heart failure right here at the table!"

It was those exact words, *heart* and *failure*, that made something raw rise up in me, that made my own heart seize when Mom crumpled in her chair. I thought of Piper and her father, who she hadn't had the chance to know for all those years because they were broken. And Mr. McMurtry, already sick when he finally met his only granddaughter. I thought of the obituary with Mrs. McMurtry's polite face looking out from the newspaper and imagined her collapsed on the floor of the clubhouse where the banquet was held, and my breath caught. Bad things really do happen in good families, and all it can take is the wrong thing said, or not said, at the wrong time. What would happen to us if Mom died because of me?

I pushed the tissue box across the table and stuffed my

hands in my lap. "I'm sorry."

Dad was still fuming. Mom dabbed her eyes with a tissue.

"Mr. McMurtry had cancer." I said. "That's why California came here, to help him. He's having some kind of treatments, but California said it could come back, or spread, and she's trying to get her mother to come back home in case that happens because she knows her mother will never forgive herself if she doesn't fix what's broken before he goes, and it's so awful, we've been searching the woods all summer trying to find her ponies because California thinks they're still alive and if she brings them back everything will be like it was before Mrs. McMurtry died and Piper will come home, but it's a mess, such a big mess, and I keep feeling like something else is wrong and I don't know what it is, all I know is I need to help California, I have to, and you can't tell me to not be her friend anymore because I won't do it, I *won't*!"

By the time I finished I was gripping the edge of the table with both hands as if I might skyrocket to the ceiling. Mom and Dad looked at each other, then at me, then at each other again. Finally, Mom's face softened. She reached her hand to touch mine and became that new Mom again.

"I'm so sorry, Annie. I can only imagine how hard this must be for California, and for you. You've obviously been a good friend to her."

Tears fell fast and furious down my cheeks because I hadn't been a good friend, and no one knew that but me. And there was Mom, being all . . . all Mom-like without the hysteria. Like she'd been taking lessons or something.

"She knows about Mrs. McMurtry and why Piper ran away, but she doesn't know why she never came back. Do you know? Were you there when Mrs. McMurtry died?"

"I was," Dad said.

"Did everyone blame her?"

One side of Dad's mouth twitched, like the memory was too awful to think about. "Her father said some terrible things to her when it happened, but he was in shock. It was obvious Margaret thought he blamed her, but he didn't. No one did. It was tragic timing, really tragic timing. She was gone before he came to his senses and realized what he had done."

"Is that why he's been the way he is all these years? Because what he said made her go away?"

"I imagine so."

"But I asked you, both of you, every summer when we drove past his farm." My voice shook worse than my hands. "I asked you why he was that way, and you never told me."

There was this long pause when they telepathy-decided who would answer. Finally, Mom said, "You were so young when you first started asking, we thought the truth might frighten you."

"Did anyone try to help him?"

Dad grimaced. "He didn't want anyone around, Pumpkin. The last time I saw him, you were five. You were already infatuated with that farm, and I wanted to take you over. I thought seeing you might bring him out of whatever place he had disappeared to inside his head. But he closed the door on me. And that was that."

"When you went to see him this summer, did he say anything about his cancer?"

"That's not the kind of thing you talk about with someone you haven't seen in all those years."

"Did he say anything about Piper? Or what happened?"

"He didn't say much of anything except that you were welcome at his house. That's all I needed to know."

"He had to have said more. There's something wrong, something besides his cancer and Piper. I can feel it. Do you know what it is, Dad? Can you tell me?"

Dad shook his head slowly. "Don't you think all that is enough?"

TWENTY-NINE

Until that night in July, I'd always been able to count on the sound of rain pinging against the roof to put me into a sound sleep. Long into the night I stared at nothing, and at everything. The whirr of the fan, blending with the tinny sound of rain, reminded me of the metal box full of letters from Piper. Mom's words kept running through my head.

"We thought the truth might frighten you."

What other truths might California and I not know?

The next morning California was waiting for me in the paddock, pacing the fence in the rain, a blue slicker flying behind her in the wind.

"Hurry—I have the box." She grabbed the sleeve of my raincoat and dragged me inside. "It's in the carriage. We'll hide in there, but you read."

The wheels squeaked when I stepped inside, and the seats stank of mildew. California climbed in behind me and pulled the tarp closed, her face feverish. She handed me the box and a flashlight, then tucked her hands between her knees and waited, like a little kid trying to be brave before getting a shot.

I pulled out the first envelope. The postmark said *Bradford, Pennsylvania, September fifth*. Inside was a single sheet of notebook paper.

> *Dear Jody,*
> *You will never have to see me again. You were right. It was my fault.*
> *Margaret*

California shifted uneasily. "Go on."

The second letter was from Bowling Green, Ohio, sent on September twenty-first. The handwriting was easier to read than the first, but the words were every bit as melancholy.

> *Dear Jody,*
> *I suppose Kit was already buried. She was the best mother ever. I wish I could have been there to say*

good-bye. I wish I could take everything back. I'm so
sorry.

  Margaret

I ran my finger across her signature. Only two letters in, a few short lines, and already her grief choked me. California clenched her hands together, squeezing first one thumb, then the other.

"Are you okay? Should I keep going?"

She leaned back and closed her eyes. "Yup."

It took twenty minutes to read the letters written during the first year Piper was gone. I spoke slowly, treading carefully through her past. She'd got as far as Wyoming. With every word, the muscles inside my belly tugged. We were searching for something, but now it was more than just where we might find the ponies. Now we were trying to find out why she still wouldn't come back. If we knew that, we could fix it. Then maybe the farm would feel magical to her again, like California said.

I started on the next packet. The postmark was odd. I checked the dates against the letters I'd already read, and the most recent.

"Unless some are missing, she didn't write to him for two years."

Eugene, Oregon
May 10

Dear Jody,

I'm sorry to tell you I lost Hero. It was so horrible, I still can't think about it without crying. Someone thought he was a wolf and shot him so he wouldn't go after their horses.

How are Peaches and Cream? My heart aches whenever I think about them.

We both looked up at the mention of the ponies. This was the first time she'd written about them in any of the letters. I read quickly through the rest of that bundle. In each letter Piper pleaded with her father to send news of Peaches and Cream. And every letter ended with the heartbreaking words, "I am sorry for what happened, and hope someday you will love me again."

She'd been gone almost four years before she said anything about getting replies from Mr. McMurtry. By that time she'd changed her name.

Eugene, Oregon

June 15

Dear Jody,

All three of your letters arrived at the same time. Thank you, I am so happy tonight.

And thank you for leaving hay for the ponies. Maybe you can dry the corn and leave it, too? Remember how we used to play hide-and-seek in the corn field when I was little? I still remember Kit laughing so hard it made the stalks shake. Do you remember? Or do you try not to think about us? I remember always. I remember driving back from town, coming around the curve in the road, and seeing our cornfields, so green and lush. I loved our corn. I miss that too.

Love,

Piper

"Piper loved the corn!"

California put her finger to her lips. "Not so loud. Grandfather could be nearby."

"That's why he always kept it all perfect," I whispered. "He was still hoping she'd come home. It was like a sign he still loved her."

She smiled and leaned against the seat again. "She loved the corn. She loved this farm. She loves Grandfather. And me. Keep reading."

There was one bundle left. Six letters, the dates spread far apart over many years. The fourth letter held a possible gold nugget. Long after Piper ran away, she still pined for those ponies—and she told her father where to find them.

Eugene, Oregon

August 1

Dear Jody,

Thank you for writing again. I'm still hoping you'll

send me a picture of Peaches and Cream. I know they
only come up to the farm in winter, but if you look down
where I used to take them in between shows, I bet they'll
be there, eating all that lush grass. It will be a hike, but
if you could do this for me, I will not ask anything more.
Please, please take a picture. Thank you.

  I love you,
  Piper

California wiped her eyes. "I knew they were important to her. I just knew it."

"Where would she have taken them? Someplace with more grass than the farm?"

"Or different grass. It has to be somewhere they could go on their own now, not somewhere she'd have driven them in the trailer. How many more letters are there?"

"Two." I fished around inside the box and shone the flashlight on the postmarks. "From February and March, two thousand and two."

"Right before I was born," she whispered.

  Eugene, Oregon
  February 14
  Dear Jody,
    Today is the anniversary of the day you and Kit
  brought me into this world. As my own due date
  approaches, I find myself thinking about her, realizing

what it will mean to have a daughter.

In my sleep I hear Kit's footsteps coming to my room when I had bad dreams. I see her face when she planted tulips by the porch, and hear the way she laughed when the wind made them dance. I think about her leaving inspirational notes for me by the jasmine, knowing I would find them when in a poetry mood. I hope I am as good a mother as she was to me.

Harvard built a beautiful cradle for my little girl. At night I sit and rock it back and forth, practicing for when she will lie inside it. Euberthia made lovely clothes for her, everything pure white. I cannot wait to hold her in my arms.

I love you,

Piper

California hugged her knees to her chest. "I need her."

THIRTY

Rain beat hard against the roof. I waited silently, listening to the weathervane spin in the wind, smelling mildew and old leather and a hint of horse inside the dank carriage.

"There's one more?"

The last envelopes lay in my lap. "It can wait."

"No. Now. Read it now so we can get on with finding the ponies. They'll bring her home. I'm more sure now than ever."

I shone the flashlight and pulled out the last letter.

"Look!"

Inside the folded paper was a color photograph of a petite

girl with straight, dark hair, walking away from the photographer. She was moving out of some woods, toward a clearing beside water, leading two ponies. On her right was a dark chestnut with a blond tail. On the left a pale, cream-colored palomino. Ahead of them, barely visible, was the tail and back end of a large, furry dog.

California snatched the picture from me and peered at it, close up. "I bet that's Piper and the ponies, and that's got to be the dog, Hero."

"This must be where she took them in between shows, like a vacation spot. Do you know where it is?"

"No. Maybe it tells us in that last letter. Read it."

I unfolded the weary page. "This one was read more than the others. See how worn the paper and the creases are?"

"Get on with it, Nancy Drew," she said.

I sat up straight, prepared to speak with more authority, more enthusiasm. This was it. Finally, we were going to get some real answers. But the very first line sucked the life right out of both of us.

> *Eugene, Oregon*
> *March 16*
> *Dear Jody,*
> *I am shocked and saddened by your letter. This baby, my child, will be your granddaughter. Why does it matter who her father is? Why does it matter if I am not married?*

I stopped. "California, I can't—"

"Keep reading," she mumbled, her head bowed.

I took a breath and read to the end.

> *You are ashamed of me, and still blame me for what*
> *happened. I was right not to come home. Now I want*
> *nothing more than for you to know my child, and for her*
> *to know you as I did. But you've made your own feelings*
> *painfully clear. If you change your mind and want to*
> *know her, if you feel you can love her, use this post office*
> *box. If we don't hear from you after one year, I will*
> *cancel it.*
>
> > *Piper*

I flipped the flashlight off, trying desperately to think of something to say that could change the horrible, terrible message in that letter. The rain slowed to a steady hum. I listened to California breathing, and waited.

Her voice was really tiny. "Grandfather didn't want her to have me. Isn't that how it sounded to you?"

"It sounds more like he didn't approve of Piper not being married. That's not the same thing as not wanting you."

She shook her head, her skin as pale as pearls. Lifeless. "He didn't want me. He knew where we were all along. He could have come all this time. I'm the reason they're estranged, Annie. It's because of me." She shivered and rubbed her arms. "This is a horrible day. I hate this day."

"I know what you think, but I've watched your grandfather. He loves you. I promise."

I could barely hear her. "This is all wrong. I should stop interfering. Now I understand why she won't come."

I put the letter into the envelope and balanced it on her knee. She flicked it to the floor and dropped the photo beside it.

"Piper wants to come home," I said. "You know she does by the way she always talked about this farm. We're going to find those ponies. They'll be by the lake, just like in the picture. And everything will be the same as before, only you'll be here with them."

California had stopped listening. It was impossible to convince her of anything. When I left a while later, she was standing in the middle of the orchard staring toward the woods, her shoulders back, her mouth set into a straight line. Field's head was pressed against her side, his eyes closed against the last of the drizzle.

"We'll find them," I called over the wind.

She shrugged. "The dumbest part of the whole thing with Grandfather is that I already kind of love him."

THIRTY-ONE

At lunch on Wednesday Mom and Dad had this annoying discussion about stripping the old 1950s rose wallpaper from the downstairs bathroom. The redecorating project was almost complete. The sofa was back in its new hunter-green-and-peach fabric, and the chairs had been returned to their original spots. The living room felt normal again, which was comforting and odd at the same time, since nothing else in my life felt anywhere close to normal.

"I'm so happy they were able to rush the sofa for us," Mom said. "I think your mother would have approved of the new fabric." She lifted a piece of spinach from her salad and smiled.

Dad smiled back at her. "She'd be very impressed with your taste."

Mom's cheeks flushed pink. She looked at me like she'd forgotten I was in the room.

"Oh, what do you think, Annie? Do you like the new colors?"

Colors? She wanted to know if I liked the new colors of a couch when I had so many important questions running through my mind? Serious questions, like Where are those ponies? Does Mr. McMurtry love California? How do you know if someone is going to die from cancer? How can we get Piper home? And why does my heart sink every time I think about egg salad and train fumes?

When I didn't answer, Dad asked, "You okay, Pumpkin?"

"No, yes, I mean, I have a question." I opened the Story Notebook and pulled out the photograph of Piper and the ponies. "Do you recognize that place?"

Dad put on his new glasses and took the picture from me. "That looks like Margaret from the back. Is it her?"

"I don't know for sure."

"That could be her ponies, and I think I see a bit of their dog, too. Can't remember his name, but he was always with Margaret."

"Hero."

"That's right, Hero."

"Do you know where it was taken?"

He handed it back. "Sorry, Pumpkin, I don't."

There had to be another clue, another way to figure out where that specific spot was without hiking the entire perimeter of the lake. If we took that on, we'd have to do it in little sections every day. It could take a week, maybe more, to explore the whole thing. California was losing steam, and after the way she'd reacted to that last letter, facing a challenge that big could give her just the excuse she needed to quit.

I studied the image again, top to bottom, and there was the clue, almost out of sight in the back right corner: a blur of draping, green leaves sweeping the edge of the water. No trunk showing, but as far as I knew, there was only one kind of tree that could be that tall, with branches long enough to fall all the way to the ground. I showed it to Dad again.

"Is that a weeping willow in the background?"

He readjusted his glasses, then looked over the top of them and smiled. "Why, lookie there. I believe that is—good catch, Pumpkin."

"Are there any weeping willows around our lake?"

Mom shook her head. "Not that I've ever seen, no."

But Dad was grinning. "Well, actually, there is. But you wouldn't see it unless you knew where to look, and you can't get a sailboat close enough because of the lily pads."

I was about to shoot out of my chair. "Where?"

"Remember the day we went sailing, and I told you about

the place my friends and I used to camp when I was a kid? You got all embarrassed at the idea we might have had girls there with us."

Mom perked right up. "Where is this place?"

"At the south end of the lake, where it curves back into Lily Pad Land. We used to hike around from the boathouse. If I'm not mistaken, that could be the same willow that grew by the water."

"Would Piper have taken her ponies there?"

"That piece of land belongs to the McMurtrys. Most of their property is a narrow strip that runs right along the lake. That's why there are so few houses on the west and south sides."

Bingo!

I slipped the picture into the notebook and turned to Mom. "Are you going into town this afternoon? I need to go to the library."

"Your hair is going to turn blue if you keep driving like that." Mom's chin hovered inches from the steering wheel, and she gripped it white-knuckle tight. Windshield wipers swooshed back and forth on high.

"I'm happy to take you to the library, but why did you have to go today in this rain? I've offered to take you to town any number of times this summer."

"I didn't need to go until today. Besides, Dad could have driven me."

"Not with that ankle and this downpour. So much rain this summer."

"At least it's made everything really green."

I leaned my shoulder against the window and watched droplets run down the glass. My internet research didn't give me the kind of maps I needed. The library had detailed local maps, which I hoped would show the most direct route from the farm to the lake. Mom parked the car and handed me an umbrella.

"I don't need that. I won't dissolve."

"Your decision. Meet me in the coffee shop."

"Coffee shop?"

She pointed three doors down. "I need something sweet to drink."

My outing to the library had turned into afternoon tea with Mom—but she'd actually said "your decision" like she meant it. I could give her the coffee shop for that. Twenty minutes later, with a copy of a map tucked between the pages of a book on veterinary colleges, I dodged under a stream of water pouring from over the door and found Mom inside at a booth near the front.

"I got you a hot chocolate." She pointed to a thick, white mug. "I know it's summer, but you always loved it."

I slid into the seat and hid the book and map beside me. "Thanks." With the mug in my hands, I studied waves of swirling chocolate, trying to avoid eye contact with her. Now that we were sitting across a table from each other, just the two of us, I realized we hadn't spent any time alone all summer.

"I've missed you, Annie."

I tilted the cup and made more ripples.

"I want you to know I'm happy for you, about your friendship with Margaret's daughter."

She scooped whipped cream off her latte; I studied the watercolor napkins. She played with the silk flowers on the table; I glanced up. She was smiling at me, but not in a claustrophobic way, in a nice way, like she might smile at a friend.

"You're different," I said.

"I've been taking lessons."

"Huh?"

"You're not the only one taking on new challenges this summer. I've been going into the city every week to see Dr. Clementi. He's helping me work through a lot of things I should have dealt with years ago. I'm sorry—" The shop bell jingled. Mom looked past me to the door. "Oh!"

I should have known by the startled look on her face not to turn around, but I did, anyway. Mr. McMurtry stood at the counter, no more than ten feet from us, water pooling around the bottom of his big, black boots.

"Two pounds special blend, ground extra fine," he said. The salesgirl shuffled to the back. Before I could turn away, he saw us.

"Annabel." He strode to our booth, squared his shoulders, and clicked his heels together, offering a giant hand to Mom.

"You must be Vicky. I believe we met years ago."

Mom's mouth hung open, her tongue darting back and forth inside. I wanted to reach across the table and slap it shut.

"Mom," I prompted. "This is California's grandfather."

"Oh, yes, of course." She smoothed her hair and sat a little taller before holding out her hand. "So nice to see you again."

"We've enjoyed Annabel's company very much this summer," he said.

Heat rose up my neck. It was too soon after Mom found out about California. I didn't know how she would react. Or if she would say something stupid about Mr. McMurtry's cancer, or Piper not coming to the farm, or anything else that could embarrass me to the end of the earth and make that poor man feel worse than he already must feel.

"—so Catherine didn't have just her old grandfather for company." Mr. McMurty's eyes twinkled.

Mom laughed. Softly. Politely. "It's been good for Annie, too," she said. Almost like she meant it.

The girl came back and stood behind the counter, shaking a bag. "Sir? Your order is ready."

Mr. McMurtry tapped his heels and nodded. "Well, nice to see you both," he said, and turned away.

Mom took a sip of her coffee. Mr. McMurtry paid for his beans. The bell jingled again, and he stepped out into the rain. I gripped my hands together under the table to try to stop them from shaking. I'd been struck dumb. The thing I'd worried about all summer had just happened, and the earth hadn't stopped rotating. Not yet, anyway.

"I just wish—" Mom started to say. Then a light went on in her eyes. "Oh, that's it!"

She shot up from the booth and ran out the coffee shop door.

The girl behind the counter smirked. "Go figure. Some people." Then she shuffled to the back of the shop.

My stomach swirled. What was she going to say to Mr. McMurtry? What wretched timing. I grabbed her raincoat, the umbrella, my book, and the map, and waited at the cash register for the girl to come back so I could pay for our drinks. All I could see out the window was rain. No sign of Mom or Mr. McMurtry.

The girl didn't appear. I tapped the bell on the counter. *Bing-bing-bing-bing-bing!* Still nothing. Forget it—that nasty girl could pay for our drinks herself. *Some people* for real. The door flung open and banged against the wall, spiraling the bell to the floor, where it rolled under the counter. Mom burst into the shop like she'd gone mad—which, at that moment, I believed to be true. Rainwater drizzled down her face. Mascara smeared a long, thin line down the side of her nose. Her pink blouse was soaked, her khaki pants splattered in mud, and her beige shoes coated in black. I slammed to a stop.

"Well, there you go," she trumpeted so loud I'm sure they heard her all the way at the library.

"There you go, what?"

The salesgirl hurried through the curtain, stopped half-way to the register, and snorted. Mom looked down at herself and laughed in this totally bizarre way, like she couldn't figure out how she'd got so wet. She laughed like we were in cahoots together. Reaching up with both hands, she gathered her hair and leaned to the side. With one swipe, she wrung a mop full of water onto the floor. The salesgirl backed away. I didn't blame her. Mom looked positively insane.

"I tried to catch up to him." She was straining her face muscles, trying not to laugh.

I covered my mouth with my hand. "Oh, no, what did you do?"

"I ran right through a puddle—"

Acid shot from my stomach to my throat. "You—"

"—and I called his name, Jody. His name is Jody, and—"

"Please tell me you weren't rude."

"Well, he stopped, and right then the Murphys' teenage son drove his brand-new Lexus between us, and we both got soaked." She flung her arms in the air.

"If you were rude—"

"Imagine buying your teenager a Lexus."

I took a step toward her. "Mom, what did you say to him?"

There was a pause, like she was confused and trying to figure out what just happened. She shook herself, laughed softly, and snatched her raincoat from me.

"Oh, hush, Annabel," she scolded, but not in her usual disapproving way. More in a silly-little-girl-that-I-love way. She smoothed her hair and put the raincoat on over her shoulders. "I wasn't rude. I was trying to think of something nice to do for him. I invited California to dinner."

"You what?"

"She left on a trip with her mother today and won't be back until Tuesday, so she's coming next Wednesday. Do you think she'll like leg of lamb?"

THIRTY-TWO

With California gone through the weekend, I was restless and cranky. On Friday I went to the farm to check on Field, but Mr. McMurtry was in the backyard with him. I left without saying hello. The beach held no appeal. I didn't want to sail, and was still avoiding Tommy and everyone else who had been here the night Mom found out about California. Dad was getting fidgety himself, still laid up. It would be weeks before he could play tennis again. I tried to write about Scout and Liberty, but nothing good came out. Page after page went into the trash.

Where had California and Piper gone? Maybe that last

letter had been too much after all. Would she go back to Oregon without saying good-bye?

Saturday broke the record for heat and humidity. Mom moved the fan into the living room, where Dad and I were playing chess. "Anyone for iced tea?"

I pulled up my braids and circled them on top of my head, waving my hand along the back of my neck to cool off. "Me, please. Checkmate, Dad. I won again. Stop letting me win—it's no fun."

Mom came back with a glass of ice, sliced lemons, and a pitcher of fresh tea. "You know, Annie, shorter hair will keep you cooler."

Every summer Mom tried to get me to cut off my braids. "It will be so current," she'd say. Like I cared. Current-schmurrent. I always refused, then walked away holding one fifteen-inch braid in each hand, the lifeline to my identity. But this time I didn't say no. I had an idea.

"At the library there's a poster for Locks of Love. You know what that is?"

Mom perked up. "Isn't that where you donate your hair to be made into wigs for cancer patients?"

"Yeah. I was thinking about doing it, in honor of California's grandfather."

"Pumpkin, that's a really nice idea."

"That's lovely," Mom said. She was already reaching for the phone. "I'll call the salon—"

"Hold up, Vicky. She didn't say yet whether she was ready."

Mom stopped and clasped her hands in front of her. "Oh, right, of course."

The two of them watched me, waiting. I already knew I was going to do it, but the power of making them wait was too perfect to give up, so I dragged it out, looked quizzical, played with my braids, and tucked my face so they couldn't see me smiling. I let it go on for a good two minutes before finally saying, "Okay, yeah, I decided. I'll do it."

On Tuesday, after the longest weekend of all weekends, Mom and I drove to town to discard the last visual reminder of My Life Before This Summer: two braids I'd worn almost every day since kindergarten. Mom almost choked when I told her she couldn't come in with me.

"What? Why not? This is a big moment in your life."

"Because I really want to do this on my own, Mom." She stared at me like, if she did it long enough, I might change my mind. "You'll be the first to see it when I come out, though."

She slunk down in the seat and held out the credit card. "All right."

An hour later I walked out of the salon with two braids inside a lime-green plastic bag, instructions on how to donate them, and my hair cut thick and bouncy so it barely brushed against my shoulders. I'd even let them cut soft side bangs to puff out of my eyes if I wanted. Mom didn't say a word, just smiled and hummed all the way to the post office to send my hair away.

As we passed the farm on the way from town, I caught sight of two legs and feet hanging from an apple tree. California must be back. Why hadn't she called me?

The phone was ringing when we got home. Mom grabbed it. "Hello ? . . . Oh, yes, Jody, it was good to see you, too. We're looking forward to California coming to dinner."

Mom looked at me.

"She's not here. Let me ask Annie if she knows." She held her hand over the phone. "Mr. McMurtry can't find California. Do you know where she is?"

I knew exactly whose legs and feet were hanging from that tree we'd driven past.

I shook my head no.

"I'm sorry, Jody. We've been in town today, and Annie doesn't know, either. . . . Yes, of course, we'll call you right away. I've got your number on caller ID. . . . Yes, good-bye."

Twenty minutes later I was in the orchard. The legs and feet were gone. I ran as fast as I could to the river, excited to tell California what I'd discovered. She was slumped beside the old pine bough shelter we'd made when we first got Field.

"Hey," I said. "Your grandfather called our house for you."

"He can call anyone he wants," she grumbled. "I'm done with him." She made a heart shape in the dirt with a stick and stabbed it in the center so the twig broke in two. "You cut your hair."

I brushed my fingers up from the nape of my neck. "I donated it to Locks of Love in your grandfather's name."

"Puh."

She didn't look like she cared much what I did with my hair or her grandfather, but it would have taken a whole lot of something wonderful to set me right in the head if that last letter had been written about me.

"How was Piper?"

"Spectacular." She wiped sweat from her face with the hem of her T-shirt, leaving a tawny stain on the fabric and dark circles under her eyes. "Super-duper, like everything else in my life."

Waiting for California's mood to change could take hours, or it could happen in the blink of an eye. The news I had for her was about to burst right out of me.

"Well, guess what really is super-duper?"

She barely glanced up. "Hmmm?"

"I think I know where that place is in the picture. My dad used to camp there when he was a kid. I got a map at the library so we can figure out how to get to it."

I pulled the map from the pocket of my new size-five shorts, a whole size larger than the ones that kept falling off at the beginning of summer.

"Where is it?"

"At the south end of the lake, where the lily pads grow," I said, pointing to the spots I'd marked with a red Sharpie at the library. "It should be right there, and here's the farm, over on this side."

California studied the map, her face crinkled but her eyes glued to the paper. "Can I keep this?"

"Sure. When you come to dinner, we'll figure out how to get there."

"I'm coming to dinner? Since when?"

"Oh, Mom and I saw your grandfather at the coffee shop last week. She invited you for tomorrow night. Didn't he say anything?"

"Puh. No, but we're not speaking," she said, pulling her gray T-shirt away from her body. She was shrinking. The trips to the city were wearing her down. And that awful letter.

"Will you come?"

"Sure. Do you know how far it is from the farm to this spot?"

"Once we get to the edge of the lake, it's probably two miles. Getting through the woods to the water will be the hardest part, but we can do it. I know we can."

"Okay, good."

She bit her bottom lip and pushed herself up from the dirt. That was it. That's all she said. I'd waited six days to tell her the news, and she said, "Okay, good," then walked away with one hand pressed into her lower back. I wasn't sure if she'd hurt it, but something told me to leave it alone. Don't ask about her back. Don't ask about her mother. And for sure don't bring up her grandfather's name again.

At the house, Mr. McMurtry silently held open the screen door to let her in. There wasn't anything wrong with her except that last letter. It had drained the heart out of her. That was all. That had to be all.

THIRTY-THREE

The next evening Dad and I drove over to get her. I was surprisingly calm. Not a hint of throat tightening, no sign of a looming panic attack. I'd been worried about California coming for dinner, worried Mom might say something if she stabbed at her food like she was killing a beast. Mom had changed napkins twice, made Dad and me test the lamb gravy, rearranged the flowers on the table, and kept saying how glad she was we already had the sofa back. If she'd seen Mr. McMurtry's kitchen, she wouldn't have cared one lick about a sofa.

California was waiting by the mailbox. Her hair was

tied with a hot-pink, chiffon scarf trailing down her back and—thank God—she had on normal, khaki, Mom-approved shorts, and shoes. She was wearing shoes. Dad got out and opened the door for her.

"Hello, Mr. Stockton," she said. "Grandfather said to say hi." Her voice sounded raspy, like Dad's after he watched the Red Sox lose on TV.

"Nice to meet you, California."

"You can call me Catherine if you prefer. That's what Grandfather calls me."

"I'll call you whatever you want, but I kind of like California—as in the state, right?" Dad winked, and California blushed. "I'm going to be sure your grandfather has our number. Be right back. Don't tell Annie's mom I 'forgot' my crutches."

She scooted into the backseat, grinning.

"Hey," I said. "You feel better?"

"Sort of. Sorry I was such a loser yesterday. Wasn't feeling well. But I might have a plan."

"What? Tell me!"

"In a bit, I'm still sorting it out in my head."

She watched out the window for Dad to return. It sure took him a long time. When he finally rounded the corner, his head was down. He stopped and turned, staring toward the woods, then ruffled Field's neck and lumbered on to the car. When he slid into his seat, he reached over and squeezed my shoulder. The three of us were silent the whole way home.

Mom had her apron off and was waiting at the door. She held out her hand before California got to the top step and glanced sheepishly at me. "Hello, it's nice to meet you."

California pumped Mom's hand. "Very nice to meet you, Mrs. Stockton."

We stood awkwardly in the entryway, watching Dad limp his way up the steps. Mom couldn't help clucking. "You forgot your crutches. Were you okay driving?" She turned to California and explained, "This was his first time since he sprained his ankle."

"He did great, Mrs. Stockton. I'd never have guessed he was injured." California winked at Dad, and I almost lost it.

Inside, he tread gingerly to the bar and got out two glasses. "How about something to drink, girls. What would you like? California?"

Mom cringed. Visibly.

"You can call me Catherine if you prefer."

Mom fluttered her hands around her face. "Oh, no, I don't mind. I'll call you whatever you want—"

"Call her California," I said.

That settled Mom, and she went back to the kitchen. Dad poured us each a birch beer, and we sat side by side on the newly covered sofa. My foot tapped the floor. Dad startled me when he spoke.

"How is your mother?"

I splashed soda on my lap. Mom rushed in from the kitchen.

"Yes, how is your mother?"

Oh, no, here it comes—

California took a sip and placed her glass on a coaster. "She's fine, thank you. She took the summer off from work, so she could be nearby."

"Nearby?" Mom asked.

The Interrogation was coming, the one about the person Grandmother Stockton hadn't approved of, and we all knew what that meant.

I jumped up. "Hey, want to see my room?" I signaled for her to follow me. "We'll be right back."

Upstairs, California walked around and stopped at my dresser, picking up the family photo from when I was five. "Do you still have that picture of Piper and the ponies?"

I slipped it out of the Story Notebook and handed it to her. She sat in the rocker and traced the outline of Piper's image with her finger and started to hum the Peaches-and-Cream song. Soft at first, then louder, and suddenly the lyrics came flooding back to me.

"Sing the words," I said.

"Peaches and Cream and fields of green, memories from long ago, I weep for you with broken heart, under the willow, under the willow—"

I pointed to the corner of the photo. "A weeping willow, right there. Just like in her song."

Turns out I didn't need to worry about California's table manners. They were surprisingly perfect. She sat tall and talked with Mom all through dinner, complimenting the lamb and the flowers. Afterward, she stood to help me clear the table.

"You're the guest, California. Sit," Mom gushed.

"Oh, no, Grandfather would be embarrassed if I didn't help."

"Well, isn't that nice, thank you." She glanced at Dad and smiled, then got restless and went to the kitchen, reappearing with a tower of meringue, perfectly browned, on top of her famous lemon pie.

California's eyes widened. "Oh, yummy."

"It's lemon meringue," Mom said, setting the pie on a ceramic hot plate in the center of the table. I had a moment of panic, thinking of the broken pie dish still hidden upstairs in my closet, and prayed California wouldn't even glance my way, let alone say anything about it.

"Ooooo, I've tried to make that myself, but it never comes out right. I don't know what I'm doing wrong. Grandfather eats every bite, but there is something about the lemon part that I can't get. And your crust! I've never been very good at crust, but yours looks like a picture from a pastry book."

California sat back in her chair and smiled brightly at each of us, one at a time, like she was full of yellow lollipops and had nothing better to do than dole out little lemon circles. I didn't know whether to laugh out loud or reach across the table and shake her. The teakettle made a *sssssssssssss* noise in the kitchen. No one moved.

"That's so interesting you like to cook, so . . . unexpected," Mom said.

"I cook for Grandfather. He says I'm quite accomplished."

"How nice," Mom said, pleasantly bewildered.

The kettle full-out whistled like it was going to blow its top.

"I would be happy to teach you. Annie has no interest in cooking, but if you like, we could make a pie together."

"I would like that very much. Thank you." California shot an are-you-satisfied glance in my direction.

The kettle and I were both about to blow. I ran to the kitchen and grabbed it off the burner; put tea bags, cups, cream, and sugar on a tray; and stepped back into the dining room just in time to hear California's voice booming.

"Could Annie spend the night at my house this Friday? It's a full moon, and Grandfather has a telescope. I thought it would be good timing. Would that be all right with you? Grandfather has already given his permission."

Oh-my-gosh-oh-my-gosh-oh-my-gosh . . . My feet were stuck to the floor. The tray shook in my hands. The cups clattered in their saucers. The room was electric. Mom wouldn't be able to contain herself. This would be more than she could bear. I was about to be totally and completely embarrassed. But then Mom looked at Dad. Dad shrugged and shoved the knife into the pie. Mom held her dessert plate out and said, "Yes, I think that would be all right."

Later, Dad waited in the car while I walked California to her door.

"What was that all about? You totally converted Mom— she's letting me spend the night at your house. Where is this telescope?"

"There's no telescope. Come at seven. And bring long pants." She patted the pocket of her shorts where the map poked out the top. "I made our plan. We're going to hike that lake in the full moon. We're going to find that willow."

THIRTY-FOUR

California was in a mood Friday night, worse than she'd been the day we read that awful letter. Mr. McMurtry was edgy, too, going in and out, from kitchen to grill and back. He'd buried ears of corn in the coals and kept turning them over and over and over like he had OCD. He rearranged the steaks over the fire so many times it was a wonder they cooked. Whenever he looked like he was about to say something to California, she turned away. It was the second time I'd been in that kitchen with them and felt so awkward.

We were halfway through the meal before anyone spoke.

"Annabel, I told your father I would send corn home with you."

"Thank you, it's delicious."

California poked at her potato and pushed a piece of steak around on her plate.

"Catherine—" Mr. McMurtry held out the vitamin bottle. She rolled her eyes and dropped it on the table.

"Drink your milk, too," he said.

"It's not even like real milk. It's from a jug."

Mr. McMurtry set down his fork and shook out three pills. "I'll get you water, but you will take these."

I ate all my steak, the whole potato, and an ear of corn. Mr. McMurtry ate two of everything. California barely touched hers. She didn't even care when he brought an apple cobbler hot from the oven. She was still mad.

"Oooo, yummy." I nudged her under the table.

"Have some cobbler, Annabel." Mr. McMurtry handed me a wooden spoon.

"Annabel, Annabel, Annabel—" California muttered. "Why can't you call her by her real name?"

"Actually, Annabel is my real name. Annie is a nickname."

California shoved her spoon into the middle of the cobbler and grunted. "Whatev."

After dinner we took a pack of cards from a drawer and went to her room. She threw the cards on the night table, flopped down on her bed, and put an arm over her eyes. "Can you turn out that light? I need to rest before we go." Within minutes her breathing had evened out. She was asleep.

Over the summer the sun had changed the color of California's hair. It was still thick, almost wiry, and usually bushed out like she'd stuck her finger into a light socket. But now, instead of straw yellow, it was this weird, see-through color, like chlorinated swimming pool hair. That's all I saw when she shook me awake a few hours later—white stuff waving around in the dark.

"It's time," she whispered.

"What?"

"Grandfather's been asleep for almost an hour. It's time to go. Come on." I could tell by the energy in her voice she'd rallied again.

Somehow, I managed to climb out the window without knocking a lamp this time and waking Mr. McMurtry. After landing with a thud, we took off running around the back of the house. Halfway down the hill California stopped and pointed to the golden moon suspended in the sky like an ornament.

"A full moon to light the way. This is the perfect night. I can feel it, Annie. Can't you?"

All around us knee-high grass, washed in gold, waved us on. California smiled that big-tooth grin that always made me giddy. Her cheekbones rose sharply, hollowing out her face, and her eyes sank at the corners. For the first time, I saw a bit of her grandfather in her.

"Hey!" She pointed behind us to where Field hobbled down the hill with Lacy close on his heels, flapping her wings and running side to side, squawking, *Wait-for-me, wait-for-me!* "She's so smart for a dumb old chicken."

At the river we picked up supplies she had stashed inside the tree: a lantern, a compass, a flashlight, two bottles of water, a packet of homemade brownies, and two ham sandwiches.

"You'll get hungry on this journey, for sure." She hoisted the backpack over her shoulder. "We can take turns. I'll carry first, and when I get tired, you take it."

The way she said it made something warm and sunny burst inside me. Our friendship had changed everything. It was more than just for now; we had a future as friends. Best friends, forever. Standing there with California, next to our tree, by our slice of the river, with that brilliant moon overhead and the ultimate adventure ahead of us, I 100 percent believed the only way the night could end would be with our finding the willow and the ponies.

"You're the leader. I'm here for you."

California held the lantern up, and the four of us turned south in a peculiar parade: Hippie Farmer Girl, Dreamy City Girl, Half-Crippled Stray Dog, and One Still-Ugly Chicken.

The moon was straight over the top of us when things started to go bad. We were so deep in the woods, I was already getting nervous about the whole adventure. But California was silent and determined. I knew better than to say anything. Every hundred yards or so she stopped, held the lantern close to the map, checked the compass, and mumbled to herself before changing course. The trees were so thick, moonlight barely broke through. Lacy had wandered off, but California was so fixated on getting to the lake that she didn't notice. I was so fixated on making my way over rocks and rotted logs and other assorted booby traps that I didn't see her hunched over in front of me until I crashed into her. Vomit splashed onto dried leaves.

"Oh, God, you're sick."

"Stop. I'm fine."

"We should go back."

She moved off without another word.

After another hour, when tears pricked my eyes and I just knew we'd never find our way out of those woods, she gasped and pitched to the left, heading down an incline. The trees thinned. Light broke through from overhead, and we passed out of total darkness, onto a spongy bank at the edge of the lake. About ten feet from the water, California fell to her knees, tilted her face to the sky, and cried, "We made it!"

Her words echoed. The moon spread a blanket of yellow over the lake so each tiny, blue-black wave danced with a sparkle of gold. I touched my cheek to be sure it was real, that I was standing in the light of something so beautiful.

Neither of us uttered a word. There wasn't anything to say. We'd made it through the woods, all the way to the lake. The first hurdle in reaching the willow.

The clouds played hide-and-seek with the moon, and silvery shadows turned California's skin as pale as cooked egg whites. She lay down and curled on her side in the grass, lost in her own thoughts. The flesh under her eyes pooled into wrinkled mauve shadows. Tiny bits of dried paste flaked off her skin and fell like dandruff. Makeup? Why would California wear makeup? The middle of my chest burned a warning. I pressed my fist against the pain and turned to watch the water lick gently at the edge of the earth.

After half an hour of silence I lifted the backpack off her shoulders. "My turn. Come on. We've got a willow tree to find."

The going was easier out of the woods, but California struggled to keep up. Every once in a while she mumbled something, or sniffled, or let loose a tiny whimper. I waited silently for her, ignoring the worrisome thoughts cluttering my mind, and soldiered on. We had to find that tree before daylight.

Field whined. I turned, searching for him in the dark. "What's wrong, pup?"

The flashlight lay on the ground. California was bent at the waist, arms stretched and palms flat against a tree. She threw up again, wiped her mouth, picked up the flashlight, and said weakly, "I'm fine. Keep going."

She wasn't fine, and I wasn't going one more step until she felt better. I held the lantern high, marched down to the water, and pointed to a level spot.

"Sit," I said. "I'm hungry."

She lay on her back in the grass. I unwrapped a sandwich, picking at the crust, stalling to give her time to get her strength back. When she started talking, her voice was quiet and raspy.

"This is how Piper taught me about the universe. We'd lie outside under the stars, and she'd tell me everything." She paused and took a few deep breaths. "Obviously she didn't tell me everything, because she forgot to mention I had a real, live grandfather."

After a few minutes she said, "Piper's not strong inside, not like you and me." Another pause to catch her breath. "She can split firewood better than Grandfather, but inside she's like china. Her heart shatters if she thinks you're mad at her. She needs to come back before it's too late. We can't pretend anymore."

Her voice had gotten so quiet, I wasn't sure I'd heard her right. Fear inched its way into the center of my chest. I don't know if I have ever been so scared as I was in that moment. Deep down, life-or-death scared. I tapped her arm lightly.

"We need to go home. I promise, I'll come back and find the willow. But you need to get home."

She pulled away. "Stop it."

She started talking again, not to me, but around me.

Her words made my panic rise. Not the kind that closed my throat—nothing that simple. Panic that made me want to run away and leave her lying there in the grass by herself. She frightened me.

"I never realized it." Her eyes were strangely luminous. "All this time I wanted her here, but she's been everywhere: the house, the woods, this lake—"

Tiny tears trickled from the corner of her eye, leaving a wet trail like chipped diamonds along her temple. I wanted to reach over and wipe them away, and wipe the sticky hair from her forehead, but she was too intimidating, too un-California-like. I didn't know her anymore. She crossed both hands on her chest and closed her eyes, like a corpse. A chilly breeze swept across the lake. Goose bumps popped along my arms.

"California, I have to ask you something—"

"Shhhh, don't."

She drummed her fingers along her chest. The night closed around me, and everything turned black, so black I could only see her face, ghostly white, rising from the earth like a giant mushroom. I wanted to go home. I wanted to tear through the woods and crawl through her bedroom window and pretend this had never happened, that I'd never seen her this way. I wanted to gather eggs in the morning and eat pancakes in the kitchen and climb the apple tree and laugh and talk about dumb, totally meaningless things that meant nothing to anyone except the two of us.

And for the first time in years, I wanted Mom. Because right then, seeing California lying out under that moon, there was no way to ignore the horrible, awful truth.

"We can't go back, Annie. It's too late."

"We can—"

"Stop!"

I did.

I stopped talking.

I stopped wishing.

I stopped breathing.

"Annie," she whispered, and this time she reached out not to shush me, but to take my hand in hers. "Annie, it's not Grandfather. It's me."

THIRTY-FIVE

The shock of her words stilled me. My hand crumpled inside hers. "What?"

"The drug trial, it's me. But it didn't even matter. The cancer had already spread."

"You're lying."

She turned her head enough for me to see the truth. The beige makeup that had pooled into clumps was meant to hide faint purple circles under her eyes, and discolored skin. The grief she'd held in for so long bubbled up and spilled from every pore. Her clothes were draped over a gaunt body, and I was ashamed. I should have seen, I should have known, but I was too busy worrying about my own little world to recognize something so great in hers.

I yanked my hand away and slammed it, fisted, into the ground, wailing so loud owls flew away. How do people keep breathing after hearing something like this? How do they ever walk a straight line again, or brush their teeth the same as before? How would I pick which cereal to eat for breakfast, or decide whether to paint my room blue instead of green? How could I keep walking, talking, laughing, crying, sleeping when everything else had stopped, when everything good was stolen in the breath it took to utter two words? *It's me.*

"Why didn't you tell me? You lied! I thought we were friends."

"Piper and I leave tomorrow."

The air sucked out of my chest. "No! It's too soon."

"Not too soon . . . almost too late."

"Where are you going?"

"Philadelphia."

"Philadelphia? What's in Philadelphia?"

"Hospital—"

"For what? Why? Are they going to fix you?"

She didn't answer. I had to get Mr. McMurtry. We couldn't go on. Mr. McMurtry would come. We'd get her home and put her to bed, and I could tell Piper about the ponies tomorrow. Piper and I could find them, and California would be so happy, maybe she'd even get well.

"I'm going back to get your grandfather—"

"No." She inhaled sharply. "Find the willow. It's our last chance. Please—"

"How am I supposed to leave you alone to go find it?"

"The same way you were going to leave to get Grandfather—" She spoke each word between tiny gasps.

My throat tightened. Panic made me jump up and pace, rubbing my chest, trying to make the pain go away. Her back was hunched, and through her T-shirt I could see the outline of her spine. She was so skinny. All summer she'd been worried about me and how I needed to eat, and all that time she'd been so sick and I hadn't even paid attention.

"Have you been sick all summer?"

"Not when I first came. I was in remission. Annie, I'm too tired," she said, her voice barely a whisper. "Please—"

I looked into the black night and shivered.

I'm tired, too. And scared. What if I get lost? What if I can't find you again? What if you die?

California could die, and the only thing she wanted was to reunite her mother and grandfather. "Okay," I said. "I'll go."

I set the lantern in the grass and left her curled on her side to rest. Field sat at attention, guarding her. Which way? South, in search of the willow? Or north, in search of help? North. That was the right thing to do. She was asleep. She'd never know until I was back with Mr. McMurtry.

After a few steps I stopped. She wanted me to go south, to find the willow. If we found the ponies, we could re-create the magical world Piper had grown up in, and maybe she'd stay. Piper didn't even know how much California wanted that. It's all she wanted, and I finally understood the real reason why.

I searched for the North Star, the one Mom said was special when I was little. I found it and wished to feel her arms circling me like when she read to me in the rocking chair. I wished to feel her hair tickle my cheek and inhale the fresh, clean smell of her Ivory soap skin. California was right. For all her spreadsheets and rigid ways, Mom was there for me. Every day, every night, whether I wanted her or not. And she was trying so hard to make me happy.

California's family was all broken into pieces. Mr. McMurtry had never hinted she was sick. He'd kept her secret. What did he feel now, knowing he had missed all those years with her? What would he tell me to do?

Whatever she wants.

Pivoting south, I ran past her and kept running, running, running along the edge of the water until I was out of breath and every string that had ever been around my neck had fallen away. The earth curved on a narrow path between the water and the trees growing snug against each other to my right. An owl screeched, and fear pricked at the back of my neck. Wings flapped over my head. The owl shrieked again, so close I ducked to the ground, holding the flashlight up like a baseball bat. The noise faded deep in the woods. The moon sailed from behind a cloud and shone full and bright across the lake. Ripples of water splashed against a long dock jutting out into the dark. At the end, a rowboat swooned up and down, its oars already in the riggers like someone had left it for me. I ran down the dock, untied the rope, climbed in, and started rowing.

The lantern flickered in the grass beside California. I climbed out of the boat and waded through knee-high water, the tide and my soaked jeans tugging at me, trying to pull me under. I pushed through. Nothing was going to keep me from saving her.

Looping the rope around a clump of cattails, I clawed my way up the bank. California lay on her back, her chest slowly rising and falling. Drops of sweat dotted her forehead. *Oh, God, please, let her be okay.*

"California?"

Her eyes flipped open, and she stared at the sky. "Did you find them?"

"Not yet, but I found a boat. I came back for you."

"A boat?"

"Yeah, a rowboat, tied to a dock."

"You stole a rowboat for me."

I pushed hair away from her mouth. "Yeah, if you put it that way."

"We'll bring it back, right?"

"Sure, we definitely will."

I carried her, piggyback style, through the water, holding tight to her arms.

"You're not so skinny anymore, Annie-girl."

"Nope, all that food you've been forcing on me. You're going to make me fat."

"Yeah, you're going to get fat."

She gave a weak laugh, and I rolled her into the boat. Field plunged through the water and scrambled up behind her while I slogged back for the backpack and lantern, then yanked the rope loose from the cattails, climbed in, and turned the bow south.

With Herculean strength I rowed against the tide, the silence broken only by the dip, dip, dip of the blades. My armpits burned, my chest squeezed tight, and with every pull I let loose a desperate cry. What was I doing? Trying to find a phantom willow tree? Searching for two ponies that might only be alive in California's mind? Blindly doing whatever she asked me to do?

No. I was doing what she would do for me. Anything. Everything.

Scanning the shoreline, I squinted, searching the earth, nothing but darkness between us. My arms and chest were on fire, my heart a vise stealing my breath, until finally I couldn't pull one more time and dropped the oars to let the boat drift.

Up ahead, a ribbon of sky changed, ebony to silver. I rubbed my arms and hiccuped away the last of my tears. When I reached for the oars again, the first hint of peach was beginning to mingle with the gray. The border of the lake took on a real shape. I could make out the tops of the trees and the bottom, where their trunks met the ground—black against green. Wood in hand, I rowed harder, faster toward the blooming light, toward a place where the earth arched and curved, then spun into an almost perfect circle.

Water lapped lazily over flat lily pads. I skimmed the paddles lightly over the surface to keep them from getting tangled in the stems. The gray-and-peach sky gave way to yellow, glowing on a piece of land no bigger than the paddock at the farm. Close to the woods the parcel was covered only in thick, marshy grass. But near the edge of the water, a lone, pale tree stood guard, its long, thin branches spreading wide at the top, falling into the graceful curve of a hoop skirt against the grass of the tiny meadow.

The willow.

THIRTY-SIX

The warmth of a summer dawn never felt better than when I burst from the woods and ran up the hill toward Mr. McMurtry's house. Every muscle burned from rowing the entire way across the lake, panicked I wouldn't find help fast enough. I'd carried her, barely conscious, from the boat to the edge of the woods. Field stayed behind to guard her.

A black-and-white police car was parked at an angle in the driveway, its red lights flashing. Dad stood next to it, a crutch propped under each arm. Mr. McMurtry paced in front.

"Help!" I waved my arms and stumbled into the grass. "Help!"

Mr. McMurtry ran down the hill. One of the policemen sprinted ahead of him and got to me first. I dropped into a heap.

"My name is Officer Barcus. Where is she?"

"She's . . . we . . . I . . . ."

The others caught up. Mr. McMurtry grabbed me by the shoulders and shook, his face inches from mine. "Speak, child, where is she?"

Dumbstruck, I jumped up and ran back into the woods with Officer Barcus right behind me. It took so long to find where I'd tied the boat, but California was still there, sitting with her back against a tree, her face the same ash color as the trunk. Officer Barcus felt her pulse, walked a few paces away, and talked into his walkie-talkie. Mr. McMurtry knelt next to California, cradling one of her hands in his.

"Oh, good God, Catherine, what have you done?"

Officer Barcus came back and lifted California in his arms. "Let's go. An ambulance will meet us at the house."

"Is she—"

"We have to hurry."

The whole way back, Mr. McMurtry trotted beside Officer Barcus, one hand placed on California's forehead. "Stay with me, Catherine. Stay with me," he said between pants and sobs. "You can't do this, not like this, no—"

"She's okay," Officer Barcus said. "We're going to get her there in time."

Dad and two men were waiting at the bottom of the hill with a stretcher. The men strapped California down and carried her up the hill to an ambulance waiting in the driveway. Mr. McMurtry jogged next to them, holding his hand over her heart. The last thing I saw were her feet going into the ambulance. She only had on one shoe. The other was still in the bottom of the rowboat I'd stolen to try to save her.

Mom stripped away my wet clothes and helped me into a clean T-shirt and pajama bottoms. Dad tucked me into bed and pulled the covers up snug. Both of them were silent, but their faces told me they were frightened. I don't remember much else except for Mom mumbling something about my "mental and physical state." They took up opposite ends of my bed while I cried myself to sleep.

It was already dark when I woke up. Mom had pulled the rocking chair up close and rocked gently, the quilt spread over her lap. When she saw me awake, she smiled and touched my arm.

"Have you heard anything?"

She shook her head. "Dad went back and fed the dog, but no one was home. One of the chickens was outside the pen, but he couldn't catch it."

"Lacy, she came back—"

I rolled over to face the window and cried until my body

was empty. The rest of the night I flipped from side to side, back to front, cold and clammy to hot and sweaty. I kicked off the covers, then asked for more blankets. My throat burned. I couldn't swallow. Every muscle ached, and my head pounded.

In the morning Mom swiped my forehead with the thermometer. "One hundred and one."

"Let her sleep through this," Dad said.

They gave me a spoonful of orange-flavored medicine, then laid me back in bed. Dad wiped damp hair away from my cheek and kissed my forehead. "As soon as we have news, we'll wake you."

By late afternoon my fever had broken. Mom helped me shower and put fresh sheets on the bed. Dad brought me tomato soup and a crispy grilled cheese.

"I thought you liked them burned, since that's how you always feed them to me." He winked.

"Have you heard anything?"

"No, but I left a note on the back door. We'll hear soon, I'm sure."

"Can't you go to the hospital and find out?"

Mom and Dad looked at each other. Dad said, "We need to give them some privacy. If we don't hear anything by tomorrow, I'll go."

Everything was turned upside down. Nothing was the way it was supposed to be. Dad gathered me in his arms and rocked gently, my head against the crook of his neck. "Shhhh, Pumpkin, go back to sleep. Everything is going to be okay."

"No it's not. Nothing's going to be okay ever again. I wish I didn't know."

It was dark when I woke up. The green numbers on my clock flashed ten seventeen. I'd slept off and on for a day and a half. I went in search of Mom and Dad and, at the bottom of the stairs, saw them through the living-room window sitting together on the deck, their legs draped over the edge. Dad was holding the firefly jar, and Mom was batting her hand at something around her face. Dad turned to her, and his lips moved. Mom smiled and rested her head on his shoulder. He put down the jar, draped an arm around her, and kissed the top of her head.

I watched them sit together like that for a few minutes, then, without bothering them, went back upstairs and crawled under the covers, feeling safer than I had in a very long time.

Mom and Dad were watching me. I jolted upright. "What's wrong?"

"Honey—" Mom choked up. Dad moved to the edge of my bed and put one hand my knee.

"What's wrong? Tell me! Where's California?"

"Pumpkin, she's—" He pulled my head against his chest and rocked. "They've taken her to Philadelphia, to a hospital that specializes in children's cancer—"

"Will they save her?"

"They're trying, Pumpkin. They're trying."

I lay against my pillow and stared at the ceiling. "Who's with her?"

Mom took my hand in hers. "Both her mother and grandfather are there. That's why we know, because Mr. McMurtry called and asked if you would take care of the dog and the chickens while he is gone."

"Field, oh, poor Field, he probably doesn't understand. Yes, I'll go. I'll go right now. He must be hungry." I pushed my blankets away and tried to get out of bed, but Dad held me back.

"Field is fine, Pumpkin. He's not hungry. He had one of Mom's famous egg sandwiches this morning, which he seemed to like very much."

"You took him an egg sandwich?"

"Not really," Mom said. "He ate it downstairs. He's here, honey. Dad and I brought him here for you."

"Here? He's in our house? You let him come inside?"

"It was Mom's idea." Dad winked at me and squeezed Mom's hand at the same time. "He has to stay downstairs, but he's waiting for you."

"Mom?" I looked at her, not sure I understood correctly. "Mom?"

She didn't say anything, just wiped her eyes with a tissue and kept nodding really fast. I raced downstairs. Field lay on the rug by the sliding glass door. He thumped his tail and shoved his nose under my arm when I hugged him.

"Oh, Field, you're here. You're here. It's going to be okay. I just know it. I can feel it, Field, can't you?"

THIRTY-SEVEN

Ten days went by without a word. Nothing. Each afternoon Field and I walked to the farm and took care of the chickens, then sat side by side on the back steps. Twice we went to the river, but it wasn't the same without California. The sun didn't shine as bright, the path felt dirty, the oak leaves hung limp in the August heat. Even the river water we used to swim in looked murky. The chickens were quiet and only laid a few eggs. Mom used them to make a lemon meringue pie. California was right—we practically needed sunglasses, the curd was so yellow.

On the eleventh morning I woke to the sound of the rocking

chair creaking against the floorboards. Brilliant sunshine spilled through the window, turning my whole room the color of a daffodil. I lay still, my eyes only open a slit. Someone—who was not Mom or Dad—pushed with her toes to keep rocking. Her feet barely reached the floor. The hands folded in her lap were tiny and childlike. I knew it was Piper, even without any trace of California's sturdy bones or yellow hair.

"Hi, Annie."

"Is California—"

"We brought her home last night."

I rose up on my elbows. "She's home? She's okay?" The chair rocked faster. "Tell me."

"She's back at the farm, but no—" Piper dipped her head and pressed a tissue under her nose.

"No what? What do you mean?"

She crumpled forward and didn't answer.

"Tell me! Didn't they save her?"

Every cell, every molecule in my body vibrated. I was on fire. *What? What? What?* She slowly raised her face, but she didn't have to say anything. It was all right there in her empty, frightened eyes. California was going to die.

"It was too late. The cancer had already spread long before—"

I threw off the covers and shot out of bed, balling my hands into fists. "No!"

"They couldn't do the treatments in Philadelphia, and she didn't want to stay there. She wanted to come back to the farm, to have palliative care—"

"No! She can't give up. *You* can't give up!" I screamed, inches away from her puffy face. "She never gave up on you!"

Piper stood and reached for me. "Annie, I would never—"

Mom and Dad barged through the doorway, but not in time to stop me from trying to shove both fists into the middle of Piper's chest. I pushed as hard as I could. I pushed California's disease, her lonely life, her dying spirit away from me. Piper tipped back but held tight to my wrists, keeping us both upright.

"Listen!" Her eyes were huge, the color of dark chocolate. Not a hint of California's blue. The room spun, and her face swayed. I tried to pull away to hold my stomach, to hold back the bile threatening to spew, but Piper's tiny hands held tight. "We acted as soon as we knew, but it was too late. The cancer—"

"No! I hate cancer! I *hate* it! Why didn't she tell me? Why didn't I know?"

I caved into a pile on the floor. Dad lifted me in his arms and sat on the bed, holding me snug against his chest, rocking me like a baby. The last I saw of Piper, she was leaving my room, her back hunched, her face planted in her hands, with Mom's arm wrapped around her shoulders.

The next morning Mom asked if she could drive me and Field to the farm. Her eyes were red rimmed, but the expected hysteria was missing, so I agreed. We sat in the car for a few minutes before I went inside.

"Are you nervous?"

"A little. And embarrassed. I was rude. But I want to see California."

Mom watched me struggling. "Annie, I know you won't understand this until you hold your own child in your arms, but there's nothing in the world more powerful than a mother's love for her child. Nothing."

She reached across the seat and put her hand lightly on top of mine. It was warm and soft, and for a second I felt like I was little, wrapped in the circle of her arms.

"When you go in there, remember that Piper is a mother about to lose her only child. Her life will never be the same." Her voice wobbled. "I don't know what I would do if I ever lost you."

I lay my head on her shoulder until Field whined from the backseat.

When I knocked on the screen door, Piper stood from the table, a sad smile on her lips and a wet tissue in her hand. "Annie, you came."

Mr. McMurtry was rooted to the big rocking chair, his eyes trained on the brick floor, his large, gnarled hands woven together.

"I'm really sorry for the way I acted yesterday. I was—"

"It's okay, sweetheart. I understand."

Piper poured us each a glass of water and sat next to me at the table. The only sound came from the whirring of the ceiling fan and an occasional cluck from outside.

"There are things you should know before you go see her." She studied her lap, then took my hands and squeezed. "California was diagnosed with cancer when she was ten."

Mr. McMurtry made this horrible noise, then stuffed his hand in his mouth and strode from the room, letting the screen door slam. Piper watched him leave with a steely expression. She blew a puff of air, then stood, crossed to the sink, and stared out the window.

"Regret is a terrible thing, Annie."

The sound of an ax splitting logs came from outside. *Crack. Crack. Crack.* Each time Mr. McMurtry hit another piece of wood, Piper winced. After a few minutes she exhaled a long, slow breath and came back to the table.

"Forgive me. This isn't easy. None of it," she said, pulling a wad of tissues from a box. "It was one bad cell in a million good ones that qualified her for this experimental trial. She'd been doing so well. You saw how strong she was in the beginning of summer. We were lucky to be picked. So, of course, we came."

"Why didn't it work?"

She shook her head. "The drug was to try to eradicate the few cancer cells still in her blood. It had nothing to do with where it had already spread."

"She wanted you and Mr. McMurtry to be fixed, but she said it was in case he— She never told me—"

Piper wiped my cheek with her thumb, then hugged me

close. She smelled like lavender and fresh air. Her arms were muscled and strong, but I could tell she'd already started to break inside, exactly like California said she would.

"She's always been so brave, and a dreamer, too, you know? She thought this farm was magical. She wanted to experience it the way I had. After everything she'd come through, I couldn't deny her that."

"It was magical," I whispered. "For both of us."

It was too much, watching Piper's agony and trying to hold in my own. I lay my forehead on the edge of the table and let tears drop to the brick floor.

"Annie, listen to me. California said you are so strong. She said you are fearless, that you face every challenge with more courage than anyone she's ever known. Be that person. When you go back there to see her, be courageous."

Strong, fearless, courageous. The words were for someone else, not me, except they came from California, who knew me better than anyone. I lifted my head and took the tissue Piper offered.

"I'm really glad she got to be here this summer," I said. "Even if we never did find the ponies. She wanted to find them for you, so everything would be like it was before."

The corners of her eyes sank, just like Mr. McMurtry's. "I have no regrets about sharing her with my father, letting her get to know him here on the farm. It's what I always wanted for her. I know this is impossible for you to understand, Annie, but sometimes when you're a mom, you have to do things that are really hard so your child can grow and be free."

Her voice caught.

"California wanted to be here as much as possible. If I hadn't let her come, she would have withered. You never want that. You always want your child to bloom."

She studied my face. A big sob rose from a place deep inside her, and she wilted against my chest.

"I know you don't understand, Annie. No one does. No one can—"

The screen door opened. Mom stepped into the kitchen.

"I do," she said gently. "I understand."

THIRTY-EIGHT

California looked shrunken under the sheets, colorless and frail, like a naked baby bird with see-through skin and blue veins that popped like worm trails. In only a few weeks her eyes had sunk deep into the sockets. A breeze lifted white lace curtains into the room, but even with the fresh air, I knew what I was smelling was the sickness that would take her life. I wished I could hold her cupped in my hands the same way she'd taught me to hold a baby chick: gentle but firm, so she wouldn't fall.

I sat down and watched her breathing oxygen through a tube under her nose, knowing she was slipping away and there was nothing I could do to stop it. I'm not sure how long I'd been there when she woke up and smiled a tiny smile. Her lips were so chapped I touched my own to wipe away the phantom pain.

"Hey, Annie-girl."

"Hey." I rubbed my fingers along a purple bruise on the back of her hand.

"The IV line. I bruise easily."

"I'm sorry."

"It's okay. I'm pretty sure you didn't give me cancer, did you?"

We both smiled before she drifted off to sleep. Her breathing changed, she opened her eyes and we stared at each other in silence, and she slept again. We went through that cycle several times before she said anything else.

"You're not mad at me, are you?"

"About what?"

"Not telling the truth."

"No, I'm not mad." Hot tears streamed down my cheeks, and she jiggled my hand.

"Hey, hey, Annie-girl, don't cry. Please don't cry. Hey, you wanna know something funny?"

"Sure."

"I think you're the bee's knees."

The bee's knees. Such a California thing to say. I giggled, and she smiled until her cracked lips bled. I dabbed at the blood with a tissue. That sent me into tearful spasms, so she took the tissue and dabbed my cheeks. We both started laughing, and when we were done, we cried and held tight to each other's hands until there were no more tears.

"You found the willow." Her voice was weak, barely any California there.

"We did, you and me."

"You'll take Piper, right? You'll show her we found it so she'll stay?"

"Yes."

"Will you be sure they take good care of Field?"

"Of course."

The corners of her mouth rose. She settled against the pillows and closed her eyes. A little later she woke up and pressed my hand against her chest. "Annie, what's inside your red notebook?"

I'd never brought the notebook back after the day she said it was like a binky. "It's a story I'm writing."

"About what?"

"A girl and a wild horse and the horse is hurt and the girl is trying to help it but the horse keeps running away."

"What happens in the end?"

"I, um, I don't know. I haven't finished."

"Can you finish it and read it to me?"

I nodded and grabbed a fresh tissue.

"I'm sorry I didn't tell you. I needed one person who didn't know. I wanted to be like a normal kid for the summer. You were my one normal-summer friend." A few more minutes went by and she whispered, "Thank you, Annie," before falling back asleep.

Piper came in a while later to say the hospice nurse had arrived to check California.

"Can I come again?"

"Come whenever you want."

"How—how much time—how will we know—"

Piper stroked the back of her fingers across California's forehead. "There's no way to tell exactly. But it will be peaceful, and it's what she wanted, to be here at the farm with me and her grandfather."

I leaned over to kiss the top of California's head and whispered close to her ear.

"You make my heart swing sideways."

Then I turned and ran down the hallway, straight into Mom's arms.

THIRTY-NINE

California died a week later.

It was sooner than we expected, but Dad said he thought once Piper came home, she let go. I'd gone to see her every day and, even though she never woke up when I was there, I finished my story and read it to her. I don't know if she heard, but just to be sure, when I was done, I lay the red Story Notebook on the bed next to her. Later that night Piper and Mr. McMurtry were each holding one of her hands when she went away.

The next day Mom and Dad carried a bouquet of flowers and a casserole into Mr. McMurtry's kitchen. Mom and Piper hugged, Dad put his hand on Mr. McMurtry's shoulder, then they both left without saying anything. Mr. McMurtry sat by the fireplace, head down, elbows on knees, his big, gnarled hands clasped together. He hadn't spoken to me since that awful morning after the night before.

I held out the metal box to Piper. "The letters are in here. She left them in the carriage, and I wasn't sure what to do with them, so I took them home for safekeeping."

She smiled. "It's okay, Annie. Everything's okay." She handed me a white envelope. "California left you something."

On the outside she had written *To Miss Annabel Sinclair Stockton, affectionately known as Annie to those who love her.*

Mr. McMurtry looked up with bloodshot eyes. "She wrote that a few days back, before the end was imminent. It took all her strength. Must be important."

He turned away from what must have been too painful to see and lowered his head. The envelope shook in my hand.

"Would you rather read it in private?" Piper asked.

"I think I want to go down by the river."

She winced, nodding sadly.

Field stood to follow me. By the time we got to the oak tree, Lacy had caught up. I plopped down in the sandy dip where Field's shelter had been and stared at the crooked words she had struggled to write for me. Inside was a single sheet of folded paper with only five words.

Take her to the willow.

Underneath she had tried to draw a picture of two ponies

and a tree with long, stringy branches reaching all the way to the ground. In the center of the tree, she had penciled in a faint heart. It was good I hadn't opened it in front of Piper, because I sat under that tree and cried until my stomach hurt. All my loneliness, my sadness, my memories of her laughter, her lessons, her funny words echoed through my ears. My agony poured out until nothing was left inside except quiet and still. Only then, when I felt that peace, did I stand up and walk out of those woods for the last time.

It was almost September before we scattered the ashes. Piper picked a Tuesday because that was California's favorite day of the week. She invited Mom and Dad to come with us, but Mom suggested we go—just Mr. McMurtry, Piper, me, and Field—and she and Dad would stay at the farm and cook dinner for everyone instead.

I hugged Mom in the driveway before we left. "Thank you," I whispered.

She brushed hair out of my face, put her hand on my cheek, and said, "I'm so in awe of you."

Piper drove the old Buick a mile toward town before turning onto a narrow dirt lane cutting straight through the woods. About a hundred feet down, the road ended abruptly.

"The willow is no more than a quarter mile down this path," she said, pointing to a slight opening between the trees. "Of course, you girls didn't know that, but isn't that just like California, so hardheaded and impulsive. God forbid she should ever ask for help." She rested her forehead on the steering wheel for a moment before we all got out of the car.

In the daylight everything looked different. A trail wound its way through the trees all the way down to the tiny peninsula. The willow stood tall and wide, with sweeping chartreuse branches rustling gently against the earth.

"I used to come down here with the ponies on hot summer days. It was their vacation spot. They loved it." She looked out across the lake and pointed to a white dot nestled in the green on the other side.

"The farm," Mr. McMurtry said quietly. He'd had a haircut and trimmed his beard, and on that important day he wore a jacket and slacks, like he was going to a real funeral in a church. Piper leaned her head against his chest and looped an arm around his waist. I hoped it meant she was going to stay, but she'd already told me she hadn't decided.

"It depends on where I feel California's presence the most, and I won't know that for a while. I miss her."

I missed her, too. Fiercely. I cried myself to sleep every night. Mom slept in the rocking chair next to my bed and let me cry without hovering. For the first time since I was little, she understood how to comfort me.

Piper opened California's backpack and lifted out the porcelain urn from the secret room. Unscrewing the lid, she reached inside, then handed a soft, purple velvet bag to her father. She took out another bag, this one sapphire blue, and held it up close to her heart.

"California can be with Kit now."

No one had to tell me how much Mr. McMurtry hurt. All those years he could have been a part of California's life. But he wasn't because he'd been stubborn, and now it was too late. He'd got only a tiny slice of her, only a few weeks more than me. I moved behind them and stared at the ground, wrapping my fingers around the soft fur on Field's neck, and remembered what California had told Piper about me.

Be strong. Don't fall apart. Be strong for them, and for California.

In tandem, Piper and Mr. McMurtry reached into their bags and flung their hands toward the aqua sky, letting loose a fog of ash that blew out over the water and mixed together, blending grandmother and granddaughter into one puff before disappearing into the air. Piper and her father stood with their arms touching, looking out over the lake where the people they loved had gone. Mr. McMurtry searched for his daughter's hand, found it, and held on tight. I wanted to wrap my arms around the two of them from behind, to join them together forever, but instead I closed my eyes and wished California could have seen them. It would have meant everything.

I wished I could hear her voice one more time, see her climb a tree faster than a monkey, lope through the woods with Lacy tucked under her arm, her broad knees lifting as high as a parade pony. I wished for one more kooky lesson, one more moment when she looked at me and made me feel

277

powerful. I wished for many things, just one more time.

Warmth cascaded from the top of my head, down my back, through my arms and legs, all the way to the tips of my toes. I looked up at the sky where the ashes had gone, and there she was, flying out over the water, laughing, her face full and pink again, her yellow hair all wild and free, and her big, ugly toes wiggling in the wind. She twirled her body around and around, somersaulting through a loop of the pink scarf she'd worn to dinner, until it wrapped itself around her like a blanket.

Up there California was so full of life—she blew me kisses, telling me she was free. I didn't understand and started to weep. I wanted to stay in her light forever. She pointed, telling me to turn around. When I did, I knew it was real. She had been there all along. Pushing through the long fronds of the willow were two old ponies—one chestnut with a yellow mane and blue eyes, the other a soft, cream palomino.

Right then, something bound up tight inside me broke free and sailed away. When I looked back, California was gone, but I heard her voice one last time, like a song carried off by the wind.

Good-bye, good-bye, good-bye—

ACKNOWLEDGMENTS

Writing a novel is like sewing a quilt made from scraps of love from those who believe in you. My gratitude reaches far beyond the generous and talented people here, because so much comes from random expressions or words that unknowingly ignite and inspire.

Everlasting thanks for the grace, shelter, and love of Kate, Brian, Bryce, and Brayden Jenkins, who blessed me with family dinners, wisdom, and the Happy Writer's Room;

My insightful critique partner, Betsy Devany Macleod, who always insists the best of me rise to the top;

My mother, Liz Turner, who is *not* a math professor but rather a highly creative bubble of effervescence;

To my five siblings, especially Michael, whose vicious red pen made me persevere just to prove him wrong, and Ashley, who devoted so much of herself to my dreams;

My patient and all-powerful agent, Al Zuckerman;

My dream editor, Andrew Harwell, thank you for guiding and encouraging me with the authority, insight, and patience of an editor, an educator, and a shrink;

Rosemary Brosnan, Erin Fitzsimmons, Olivia Swomley, Dawn Cooper, and all the HarperCollins teams who loved this story and made it happen;

SCBWI especially in Austin, NJ; and MD/DE/WV;

The Jackson Hole Writers;

The Highlights Foundation;

Dr. Susan Rheingold of Children's Hospital of Philadelphia;

Bethany Hegedus and the magic of The Writing Barn;

Janet Fox for answers to my never-ending questions, often sent in the middle of the night;

The writers whose use of language inspired me, especially: Victor Hugo, Anna Sewell, Laura Ingalls Wilder, Robert Frost, Mary Oliver, William Shakespeare, Kate DiCamillo, Sharon Creech, Kathi Appelt, Jacqueline Kelly;

To all who offered support and encouragement on this journey, including my sons Parker and James, Kathy Temean, Patti Lee Gauch, Teresa Crumpton, Bettina Whyte, Maureen Dorsey, April North, Kat Yeh, Brigid Kemmerer, Annabel Winters-McCabe, and Elizabeth McCague;

And finally, to my dad, Michael G. Turner, who passed away before *Swing Sideways* was finished, but whose life and death inspired so much of what is beautiful and lovely in this story. Thank you for never thinking I would be anything but what I wanted to be.

You all make my heart swing sideways.

Turn the page for a sneak peek at
NANCI TURNER STEVESON's next book

When **MAGGIE** moves with her mama
from Georgia to a tiny town in Vermont, she
meets an **UNFORGETTABLE FAMILY** who will
open **HER HEART** and change **HER LIFE.**

ONE

On a hot day in June, when all I wanted was to come back from my run and cool off in my room alone, Mama didn't even give me two minutes recovery time before she sent my world spinning. I was late for lunch, still sweaty, probably smelling like the dressing room of a high school football team, and was counting on her to send me off to shower before being allowed at the table. She barely glanced my way. Instead, she wiggled in her seat and cleared her throat twice, then stood up so fast her chair almost fell backward.

"My word, what good is central air-conditioning if it

doesn't keep you from sweating like a bronc on rodeo night?" She nervously adjusted the little lever under the thermostat on the wall, then sat down again and fanned herself with her hand. "I grew up without air-conditioning, did I tell you that? And believe me, it's a whole lot hotter where I come from than it ever thought about being here in Atlanta!"

More sweat broke out on my brow. The wiggle-and-throat-clearing thing was a sign she was about to drop some kind of bomb. I took a sip of sweet tea and swiped a napkin across my forehead. "Yup, you told me."

She shifted one more time and before I even had a chance to catch my breath, she laid the biggest kind of crazy ever right in my lap. "Did I happen to mention your daddy left you his farm in Vermont when he died?"

My daddy had been dead almost four months. I figured there must be something wrong with me because I never felt the type of devastation you're supposed to feel when a parent dies. It's not like I knew him that well. Mama had been married to Peter since I was five, and some days I forgot about my daddy altogether. But I don't think I even cried. When my best friend Irene's dog died, I was near inconsolable for days.

"No, you didn't tell me," I said. "I mean about the farm."

Mama picked up her salad fork and pushed lettuce around the plate. "Well, he did. Those kind of things always take time, but we finally got the formal documents. I had the lawyer check everything out. It's all official. There's even a trustee. And guess what else? We're going to live there for one year."

That knocked the air right out of me. She might as well have said we were moving to Siberia. Or Montana.

Her face puckered up like it did when she'd been dipping into her not-so-secret stash of Sour Patch Kids candy. "What are you looking at me like that for?" she asked.

"I'm waiting for you to tell me what you mean."

"About what?"

"About moving to Vermont. Does Peter want to go?"

Then she pretended to be really invested in her soup, stirring, sipping, studying mint-colored ripples that spread to the painted meadow around the edge of her bowl. "Oh, he's not going. Just you and me. It will be like an adventure."

"And Peter's not going becaaauuuse . . ."

Pause.

"Because he's decided to divorce us, that's why."

Then she did look at me. Right square in the eyes. And because of what I saw in hers, I didn't let the hissy fit loose that was simmering just under my skin. She was scared. I took a deep breath and picked up my spoon, drawing in the creamy sensation of chilled soup, letting it coat my tongue and hoping it would have the same soothing effect on my spinning brain.

"Peter's decided he likes that friend of his, Albert, better than us, so we're moving out and Albert's moving in. If it weren't for the opportunity your daddy's farm gives us, I might feel like discarded furniture. But, I don't. Now stop acting so shocked and close your mouth, it's hanging wide open."

My mouth wasn't hanging open because she'd implied my very proper stepfather was gay. It was hanging open because I couldn't imagine—if it was true—how he'd kept that a secret for so long. He and Mama didn't approve of homosexuality. Or at least, that's what they'd always said to me. One time at dinner, I told them about a discussion some friends and I were having at school about gay marriage. Mama had been so horrified, she'd leaned in to me and whispered, "We don't discuss things like that, sugar." Then she'd made me give her the names of all the other kids, and she'd actually called their parents.

That was my least popular week at school.

"Well, you can go to Vermont if you want," I said. "I'm staying in Georgia." I turned back to my lunch, signaling that my decision was final.

"And just where do you think you'll live?"

"Here. With Peter."

Her nostrils flared. "You, Peter, and Albert? Not a chance. We're going to Vermont and there is nothing more to discuss." She sat tall and lifted her chin, signaling that *her* decision was final.

"Why can't we stay in Atlanta and just live somewhere else? We can find an apartment near my school."

"Do you have any idea how much that fancy school of yours costs? How do you expect me to pay for something like that?"

"Peter will still pay for it," I said, my bravado fading. "Won't he?"

"He's not throwing us to the dogs, if that's what you mean.

He'll give us enough to live on, but I can't hold my head up in this town anymore, not with this—this dark shadow of shame being cast over my head."

She waved her salad fork around in the air.

"Two divorces, one from a man not right in the head, the other has decided he's in love with another man, and I'm only thirty-three years old! No, this is our chance to start over. You and I are going to Vermont and that's final."

Now it was my turn to wiggle. "But we are coming back after a year, right?"

"How can I answer that right this second? You always want answers to the most impossible questions when I'm stressed, do you realize that?"

I wasn't thirteen yet, but even I knew the truth. Any question was impossible when Mama was like this. It didn't matter if I asked how her day was, or what the astronauts on Apollo 13 ate for breakfast, it would be too difficult for her to answer. So I shut up.

"All we need to think about right now is getting through the year. It was in your daddy's last will and testament. One year, then we can sell the place and have a huge amount of money to live on the rest of our lives. Those two thousand acres are worth a fortune. That's the *only* reason I'm taking us back there."

"Well, I'm the one in school, so I vote we stay here."

"Until you are an adult, your vote doesn't count. So get over it and start packing."

* * *

Peter didn't come home until after dinner. I figured he'd planned it that way on purpose because he knew Mama was going to tell me about the divorce. Once inside, he made a beeline for his study, but he left the door open. That meant it was okay to interrupt. He sat at his computer examining a colorful graph on the screen, his back tall and stiff, his starched shirt buttoned to the top, his hair clipped in precise half circles over each ear. It was the same way he sat at the breakfast table, the same way he sat in his car, and in the stadium at my track meets. I knocked gently.

"Come in," he said.

I perched on the edge of a leather chair and clasped my hands together, hoping it made me look calm and relaxed on the outside. Inside, things were stormy.

Peter swung around. "Did you know Thomas Jefferson invented the swivel chair?"

I nodded. "You showed me when we went to Monticello."

"Yes, I'd forgotten. I did."

I shifted uneasily. The speech I'd spent the afternoon preparing escaped out the top of my head like someone had blown dandelion seeds away from the stem.

"I suppose your mother spoke to you?"

"Yes."

"I hope you don't judge me too harshly."

"No."

He dipped his head in a teeny-tiny nod and his eyes softened, like he'd really been worried I would judge him.

"I'll always see to your finances. You and your mother won't suffer for funds, and if you ever need anything, you can always call me. You know that, right?"

Then I remembered what I came to tell him. "I don't want to go to Vermont."

Silence.

Maybe he didn't understand I needed his help to make that happen.

"Can you tell her to stay? I don't mean in this house, but here, in Atlanta. I don't want to move."

Peter's left cheek twitched, just under his eye. He folded, then unfolded his hands. His cheek twitched again, and I knew right then that he wasn't going to help me.

"I understand," he said. "I really do. But she's thinking of your future. It is best."

My future? What about now? What about this very minute?

I waited, hoping he might say something else, something with more promise to it. But he didn't. Nothing. We stared at each other until his computer screen turned dark in power-save mode.

"Okay," I finally said.

"I'm glad you understand. We'll talk more before you go."

"Okay."

Peter reached out and touched my shoulder with his fingertips before turning back to his computer. I left the room feeling shocked and defeated. Really, who moves from the busy city of Atlanta to a town in Vermont so tiny you've probably never heard of it, right smack in the middle of summer, when your best friend is an ocean away on vacation and you can't even say good-bye to her?

Me. That's who.

TWO

After four long, lonely days in Vermont, we still didn't have internet. We didn't even have cell service, because living out in the boonies meant we had to have some special machine to draw in satellite signals. And I still hadn't ventured outside the big, rambling farmhouse to explore the property that was supposedly now mine.

All of the above made me cranky. At breakfast, Mama made it clear I had to change my attitude and get on with life.

"You're depressed," she said, jerking the hot sauce bottle so hard it made a red pool in the middle of her grits and burned my nose from across the table. "I am, too, but we have to deal with our current lot in life. It's only for one year. A person can do almost anything for a year, if they put their mind to it. So put your mind to it and get outside. You're pale as a ghost."

She reached out to touch my cheek, but I pulled away.

"All you've done is lie in bed for four days and read those books of yours. Get outside. Run," she said. "That always fixes you right up."

She was right. Running was the only thing, besides losing myself in a book, that guaranteed happiness for a while. So, after lunch, I headed outside, fully intending to run a mile at least. But I didn't get that far. I came to a stop at the threshold of a big red barn on the property, wondering how literal Mama'd been on the drive up north when she'd said my daddy had lived and died in that place. I was scared to go inside. What if his ghost was still lurking around, waiting for me to show up?

I put my face close to a gap in the door and cocked my ear, listening for who knows what. The only sound came from the wisp of falling dust. That's pretty darn quiet.

"Magnolia Grace?"

I launched a foot in the air and landed looking in the other direction, my hands up in front of my face. A man with skin as dark as midnight stood about ten feet away, with a black and brown dog sitting on its haunches by his side.

"Oh! Who are you?"

He took a step closer and put his hand out like he wanted

to shake, then changed his mind and stuffed it back into the pocket of his jeans.

"I'm Deacon. I live over there in the caretaker cottage," he said, indicating a small building tucked into the edge of the woods. He reached down and scratched behind the dog's ears. "And this is Quince. She and I have been watching over the place for you since your father passed."

My nerves jangled. Mama hadn't said anything about some man living on the property. That didn't mean he was lying—half the time, whatever Mama said could be all lie, part lie, or shaded truth. But you'd think she'd have told me something this important so I didn't get spooked, like I was right then.

"Does my mama know you're here?"

He nodded. "She does. I'm sorry if she didn't mention it. I didn't mean to scare you."

"How did you know my daddy?"

Deacon smiled and, when he did, a tingling sensation dropped over my head like a veil.

"Oh, that's a long story. I don't want to interrupt your visit to the barn. You go on in. We can talk another time."

I looked through the gap in the door and shook my head. "I'm not going in there. It's creepy."

"Suit yourself," he said. "That barn isn't going anywhere. Part of it is on the historic registry." He jerked his chin toward the house. "I think your mama might be looking for you."

Sure enough, Mama was watching from the porch of the white clapboard house, hands on hips, her hair already done up all blond and big. She was wearing a pair of super tight black leggings, a hot-pink polo, and drippy pearl earrings. She looked completely out of place.

"Guess I'd better go inside."

Deacon nodded. "We're right over there if you need anything," he said, indicating the cottage. "Teakettle is always on."

"Yes, sir, thank you."

I started across the gravel driveway, checking to see if Mama was mad I'd been talking to a stranger. We weren't allowed to do that in Georgia.

"Magnolia?"

I turned back. "Yes?"

"Is that what they call you? Magnolia? Or your full name, Magnolia Grace?"

"No one calls me Magnolia. I'm Maggie."

"Maggie," he said. "Okay, Maggie it is. But just so you know, to your father you were always Magnolia Grace."

At lunch I sat by the big kitchen window looking out to a grassy field that sloped gently away from the house. A crooked wooden gate hung from a fence going across the yard. Wildflowers dotted the field in no particular order—yellow and pink, orange and fuchsia, with an occasional stalk of something blue mixed in. The field stopped abruptly at the edge of a forest scattered with tall trees with white bark.

The view was so different from the manicured lawns and bordered azalea gardens I'd known back home. Atlanta felt so far away. Mama was silent while she set our food out.

"Why didn't you say anything about that man Deacon who lives here?" I asked.

She ignored me and grumbled something instead about the house not having a proper dining room. It really bothered her, even though the kitchen was twice as big as the one back home and had enough room for two dining room tables. Plus, it had an actual fireplace in the corner, made from blue-gray stones, with these black hooks inside to hang pots from, like they did in the olden days. I'd never seen a fireplace in a kitchen before.

"He lives in that old building on the other side of the barn with his dog, Quince. Have you seen it? The shed? Or cottage, I guess he called it. They call stuff by different names here, I think."

She sat down with a plunk and lay a paper towel across her lap. "Now, how would you know if they have different names for things? This was the first time you were even outside the house."

It wasn't really a question, so I didn't answer. Instead I bit into my chicken salad sandwich, put together the same way our housekeeper, Clarissa, made it back in Georgia, with chopped apples and pecans.

"Do pecans grow in Vermont?"

No answer.

"I could look it up myself," I said. "Well, if we had internet I could. Why is it going to take so long for the cable people to come?"

"Because that's the way things happen in the boonies," she said. "I can assure you, if I'd known there wasn't even a TV in this house, let alone internet, I would have made arrangements long before we left. And to think people say Southerners are slow."

"Why do people say Southerners are slow?"

Mama picked at her bread crust. "Sugar, did you wake up today and decide to ask a year's worth of questions I don't have answers to? Because that's the way it feels, and I'm not in the mood. I've got a lot on my mind right now and would appreciate a little sensitivity to my needs."

Mama's needs were always requiring my sensitivity. I grew up understanding that her needs were first and foremost in our lives. Mine came second. Or third. Or tenth, depending on who else was around at any particular moment. I shut up and studied a flock of birds that rose together out of the tall grass and flew away in unison, disappearing over the tops of the trees. A little something lonely tugged at my heart.